PHANTOM MAGIC

Dragon's Gift: The Seeker Book 5

Linsey Hall

DEDICATION

To Munger, with all my heart.

CHAPTER ONE

Sun sparkled on the leaves at my feet, and birds twittered in the trees around us. The forest was alive, but not in a way that Snow White would like.

"Do those chirps sound threatening to you?" I clutched the magical lava rock closer to my chest.

"Yes." Dr. Garriso's voice was matter-of-fact.

I laughed warily. "Perfect."

"Don't worry. I know all the booby traps that the Collector set up. We'll be fine." He hesitated. "I think."

I grinned at him, glancing at his slight figure out of the corner of my eye. I rarely saw the professor outside of his book-filled office. In his tweed coat and loafers, he didn't look like he should be trekking through the woods with me in the outskirts of Magic's Bend. But I needed his help, so here he was.

The two of us were hunting down answers about the magical rock I'd stolen from my enemies, the Shadows, and I hoped that the mysterious figure called the Collector had some.

"Thank you for taking me," I said.

"Of course. I'm just sorry that I couldn't answer your questions about that rock there." He nodded to the lump of cooled lava in my hands. "But I think the Collector might be able to help."

"I hope so." We'd recovered the magical stone from the Shadow's compound just yesterday, when I'd tried to stop them from creating the portal between Earth and the Underworld.

Unfortunately, I'd failed. Demons were currently spilling out onto Earth. We didn't know how many yet, but it was sure to be a lot. And whatever they were up to—it wasn't good. They were the "wreak havoc and cause hell" sort of demons. They'd been plotting their attack for centuries, and the day was finally here.

And I'd helped them. I'd been forced to.

So, things weren't going great.

We had to find the portal I'd helped create and close it before too many demons escaped. Problem was, we had no idea where it was located.

Fortunately, my Dragon sense had given me a lead that Roarke and I were going to pursue after I asked the Collector about the magical lava rock. We'd all agreed that this hunk of rock was important. It had powered the machine that had helped open the portal, but we had no idea how to access that power or what it could do. The magic that vibrated within it was more powerful than almost anything I'd ever felt. Even my dragon sense had tugged toward the lump of stone, suggesting that it was vital.

So I'd gone to Dr. Garriso early this morning to ask him if he knew what it was. Dr. Garriso, resident scholar at the Museum for Magical History, knew almost everything. He'd had no answers, but like any good scholar, he knew where he might be able to find some.

"Stop!" His arm snapped out, and I stumbled to a halt.

My gaze followed his, dropping to the ground in front of our feet. Though we walked through the deep woods outside of town, we were on a path.

At my feet, vines twisted and writhed like snakes. They blended with the ground so perfectly that I'd almost missed them.

I eyed them warily. "Good catch."

"I come here quite often." He dug into his pocket and withdrew a little bag. After untying it, he flung the powdery contents at the vines.

They lay still. Mostly.

We walked across. They shifted beneath my feet, making my stomach turn.

"Would they drag us into the earth?" I asked.

"Yes." He glanced toward the trees. The chirping had increased in volume, like a thousand angry little birds shrieking their rage to the sky.

"The Collector gave me protection from the birds," he said. "But you don't have it. You must run now. Follow me."

He took off down the path, fast for a man in his seventies. I sprinted after him, wind tearing at my hair, as the chirping birds hurtled from the trees. Tiny bites of pain pinged against my back. The sparrows hurtled into me.

Quickly, I adopted my Phantom form, letting the icy magic flow through me. It was a risk, since I hadn't told Dr. Garriso that I was part Phantom, but I trusted him. I'd helped save his life once, and he was the sort who would return the favor.

The birds chirped, fluttering around my head, going for my eyes. They flew straight through my head, sending a shudder through me. Thank fates I'd shifted. These little bastards were vicious. They'd take an eye rather than look at me.

A few moments later, we sprinted through a magical barrier that prickled against my skin. It was pleasant rather than painful, and I was grateful to realize that it wasn't meant to stop me—just the birds.

They stopped flitting around my head, so I pulled to a halt and returned to my human form. When I turned, they fluttered in place, a wall of feathers and beaks, shrieking and chirping as they glared at me with beady eyes.

Dr. Garriso panted beside me. "The Collector is very concerned with security."

I sucked a breath into my aching lungs. "I can see that."

The birds were effective guards. Tiny, but ruthless. They were even immune to my charm over animals.

"Come now."

I followed Dr. Garriso down the path, keeping my senses alert. The trees rustled around us, but there was no evil chirping of deadly sparrows.

The path continued, leading us to a wall of trees. The gnarled branches twisted and twined around each other, forming an impenetrable barrier that cut off our access to the path.

"Her home is just on the other side," Dr. Garriso said.

"This is a lot." I indicated the branches. "Why is she so obsessed with security? Do people want her dead?"

"No. I don't think so. But she does possess the largest collection of magical objects in the world. It's the reason she is so knowledgeable. And the reason she is so paranoid."

"Afraid of theft." Of course. So were we, at our shop. I could understand where she was coming from.

"Exactly." He stepped toward the trees. "Wait here."

I watched as he approached the wall of twisted tree limbs. He reached up, his hands as gnarled as the wood, and ran his fingertips over different sections of the bark. If it was in a pattern, I couldn't determine it. But after a moment, the trees trembled. The limbs untangled themselves and drew back, forming a gap that we could pass through.

"Don't brush the trees as you pass," Dr. Garriso said. "Poison."

"It didn't affect you?"

He shook his head. "Immune."

"How do you know the Collector so well? She's allowed you unrestricted access to her place." As soon as I asked the question, I knew the answer.

He gave me a wry look.

I blushed—we didn't exactly have the kind of relationship where we talked about our sex lives—and preceded him through the trees and onto a neatly cultivated path. Rose bushes bloomed alongside the stone walkway that led up to an old Victorian house.

The different sections were painted bright shades of blue. The yellow and white trim gave it a cheerful air. The porch was an expansive space surrounded by an intricately carved wooden railing.

And it was covered in cats. At least a dozen of them—all colors and sizes—lounged on the railings or in little beds. As a unit, they all woke and turned their heads to stare at me. Keen eyes studied us as we approached.

"The Collector likes cats?" I asked.

"Very much." Dr. Garriso gave a melodic whistle, and the cats relaxed, returning to their slumber. "They're her last line of defense."

"House cats?"

"Deadly house cats. They'd eat your face rather than look at you."

A slender black cat with yellow eyes leapt off the porch and slunk toward us, her graceful gait making her look like she was doing a sinuous strut. She rubbed herself against Dr. Garriso's legs.

"This is Mouse," he said.

"Doesn't look very deadly," I said. The little cat couldn't weigh more than eight pounds.

As if she'd understood me, Mouse bared her fangs and hissed. I had a sudden vision of her leaping for my throat.

"My apologies, Mouse." I nodded at the cat. "You're very fierce."

Mouse nodded her head, then butted Dr. Garriso's leg again. He bent down and picked her up, then led me up the wooden stairs to the porch. Mouse watched me from over his shoulder, her enigmatic yellow eyes hard to read.

The door swung open as soon as I stepped onto the front porch.

Lurch from *The Addams Family* loomed in the door. It took a moment to realize that the tall, slender man was in fact not the weird butler from the old TV Show.

"Yes?" His voice sounded like a heavy wooden door creaking open.

Scratch that—this dude was definitely Lurch.

"Bates, I've brought a visitor for Madam Melephonus."

Of course the collector was called Madam Melephonus. It was the perfect name for a woman who hired Lurch as her butler.

Bates inclined his head and stepped back, gesturing us inside.

Mouse stayed glued to Dr. Garriso's shoulder as he entered. Fortunately, the house didn't smell like cats, though I imagined that Bates was very busy with the scooper to keep the place smelling like nothing more than lemon wood polish.

"Touch nothing." Bates's voice boomed over me as I entered.

"Aye aye." I kept my gaze straight ahead so I wouldn't bump into anything.

The hallway would have been wide if not for the shelves. They lined the walls from top to bottom, stuffed full of all manner of unique objects. The magical signatures clashed with each other, making it hard to figure out what was what.

Dr. Garriso led us to a sitting room, which was just as full as the hallway. But like the hall, the space was ruthlessly organized. Madam Melephonus was no hoarder. At least, not the kind you'd see on a TV show. The place was interesting rather that cluttered and miserable.

Mouse leapt off Dr. Garriso's shoulder as we sat on the delicate settee, and she took up a perch on a wingback chair. Then she set about cleaning her toes very intently.

"Madam Melephonus will only be a moment," Bates said.

Dr. Garriso nodded. "Thank you, Bates."

I waited in silence, my gaze dancing over every object in the room. Finally, a small woman in her early seventies entered the room. Her clothes were covered in sequins of all colors, and her spectacles were rainbow striped. Between the cats, the clothes, and the colored house, you'd think she was a flighty nutjob.

But when her sharp black eyes pierced me, I realized how stupid it would be to underestimate her. And I definitely believed that these cats would eat my face at her command.

"Irv." Her voice was light but resonant, the strangest combination that was magic in itself. "Who have you brought me?"

Dr. Garriso's first name was Irv?

"A friend. This is Delphine Bellator."

"Bellator." Her gaze went up and down my body. "That is Latin for warrior."

I nodded. The name suited me. I held out the rock. "I was hoping you could help us identify this."

Her gaze flared with interest. "I could try."

She approached, so graceful that she looked almost like she was floating on air. She stopped in front of me, peering hard at my face, then at the stone, as if she were searching me for ill intent.

"Is everything all right?" I asked.

"I just like to know what I'm dealing with." She pinched my chin and scowled. "You are one of the Triumvirate. Destined to do your part in saving the world."

"How did you know that?" I pulled my chin away.

"I know things." She looked down at the stone. "Does this have anything to do with that?"

"It might."

Finally, she nodded and took the stone from me. As soon as it left my hands, I wanted to grab it back.

That stone was *important*. I didn't know why, but I knew it as well as I knew my own name.

But it didn't matter how important it was if I didn't know exactly what it was or how to use it.

From her crinkled brow, the Collector didn't know either. "I've never seen such a thing."

"That makes two of us."

"Don't be flippant." She hurried over to a table set against a window and put the stone onto the puddle of light on the wooden surface.

I grinned, liking the old bat, and watched her examine the stone with a jeweler's loupe.

"There is great power here," she muttered. "But I know not how."

Dang it. I'd been so sure that Dr. Garriso would lead me the right way.

"But if you'll let me keep it for a few days, I think I might be able to sort it out."

My mouth opened to deny her, but Dr. Garriso gave me a hard look. *You wanted answers,* it said.

I did. And as much as I didn't want to let the stone out of my sight, I didn't have time to sit here and babysit it. Dr. Garriso trusted the Collector, and I trusted Dr. Garriso.

So…

"All right, thank you for your help." I rose.

Mouse watched me with big, yellow eyes while Dr. Garriso stood. Madam Melephonus was too intent on the stone to turn to say goodbye.

"I'll see you Sunday, Ginger."

Ginger Melephonus? What a name.

I just hoped she'd have answers for me.

An hour later, after we'd made our way back through the forest, I pulled Scooter up to the curb at Ancient

Magic. The wind was brisk and biting this late in November, and I hurried in out of the cold.

Nix was hunched over a pile of books, scowling at the pages. Her dark hair fell in her face, obscuring a black T-shirt that I knew must have some kind of cartoon character drawn on it.

"Find anything?" I asked.

"Not a thing." She looked up and frowned. "There's no mention of Oriamor anywhere."

"Damn." Though my dragon sense had given me the clue that we needed to head east, toward Savannah, Georgia, I didn't know what the heck I would find there.

"Cass hasn't had any luck either," Nix said. "She called a while ago. Aethelred knows nothing. Mordaca and Aerdeca have never heard of it."

Damn. If the seer didn't know, nor did our Darklane friends, we were really screwed for info.

"Then I'm going in blind," I said.

"Not the first time."

"Nor the last, probably."

"You find answers about the rock?"

I shook my head and told her about Madam Melephonus. As I was finishing up, the door creaked open behind me. I didn't need to turn to know it was Roarke. Not only could I smell his intoxicating sandalwood scent, but I could feel his magic. It was like a comforting blanket wrapping around me. Probably because I knew he'd always use it to protect me.

I turned, unable to help the grin that spread over my face at the sight of him. As usual, he was handsome as sin, with his dark eyes and hair gleaming in the light. The black shirt and black leather jacket he wore made him look like a romance novel hero. The tough kind who beat all the bad guys, but then had time for a nice dinner and long walk.

Which was just my style.

"Any luck?" I asked him.

He'd gone back to the Underworld while I'd been with Dr. Garriso, intending to dig around for information with some of his contacts. His brother, Cade, and our friend Emile, were off looking for answers too.

"Nothing." He approached and pulled me in for a kiss. It was brief, just the press of his lips against my own, but my head spun anyway. I couldn't get enough of kissing this guy. He pulled back. "Not a single info-broker has heard a thing about a place called Oriamor."

"So it's old, then," I said. "If no one's heard of it, it's been dead centuries. Millennia maybe."

"Possibly." He frowned. "So you found nothing either?"

"Nope. I've got no idea what we're walking into."

"So, the usual, then?"

I grinned. "Exactly."

"Want company?" Nix asked. "I'm closing up for today. I can come with you, and we can check this place out together."

I turned to her. She'd stood, and yep—her T-shirt had a drawing of some kind of cat. A Japanese one. Gigi the cat, I thought it was.

Though one might assume that a cartoon-T-shirt-wearing girl would be a pushover, the ripped jeans and motorcycle boots evened out her look. Combined with her fighter's stance—she wasn't called the Protector for nothing—she was a dangerous package.

"Thanks." I smiled. "But no. Let's stick to the plan. We'll do the first recon while you keep researching. We've got invisibility potions from Connor that'll let us lie low. If it's just the two of us and there's trouble, we can get out of there more quickly." Roarke would just create an Underpath entrance, and we'd be out in a flash.

She saluted. "Aye aye."

I turned to Roarke. "Ready?"

"Absolutely. Do we need to pick up the invisibility potions from Connor?"

"Nope. He dropped them off this morning. He knows we don't have a lot of time to spare." Not now that demons were spilling out of the portal that the Shadows had forced me to create.

I followed Roarke out of the shop and to his car, which waited at the curb in front of Scooter. As we drove, I explained to him what had happened with Madam Melephonus.

"Sounds like an odd duck, that one," he said as he parked near Mad Mordecai's, our preferred Underpath entrance.

"She was. But I liked her."

"You would." He grinned. "You like the odd ones."

"I like you, don't I?"

He laughed, then pulled me toward him and pressed a quick kiss to the top of my head.

I pushed him away. "Hey, hey. No time for funny business. We've got to save the world from my screw-up."

"You didn't screw up."

"Debatable." I climbed out of the car into the chill winter air. Roarke followed and we crossed the street. I handed him one of the invisibility potions. "Let's not drink these until we know we need them. Who knows how long this will take."

"Good plan. Last thing we need is for it to wear off at the wrong time."

"No kidding." Like all magic, the potion had its downside. Sneaking into a dangerous situation and then suddenly becoming visible was a giant bummer.

By now, I was an old hat at traveling through the Underpath. I followed Roarke into the smelly alley, took his arm, and stepped into the whirlwind ether that sucked me through space all the way to Savannah, Georgia.

When we stepped out into the dark night, my lurching stomach finally settled. The air was cool here, though not as cold as it had been in Portland, and a heavy moon shined brightly on the cemetery in front of us.

"Whoa," I breathed.

Sprawled out in front of us was the creepiest, most magnificent cemetery I'd ever seen. Massive oak trees dripped Spanish moss overtop of thousands of ornate headstones and sarcophagi. Barren bushes, long gone from their summer blooms, crouched near the gleaming white tombs. Crickets and other night bugs set up a racket as the leaves rustled in the wind. The scent of dirt and water were strong.

"Where are we?" I asked.

"Bonaventure Cemetery. Largest one in Savannah. Famous, too."

"I can see why." It was a place that was so beautiful, and so strange, that people would come from all over to visit. Weird people, but people. I was one of them. "At least it's quiet."

"This isn't Oriamor, that's for sure."

He was right. There were no demons, just an eerie chill in the air that I'd bet my trove was from ghosts. "No. But I don't think we're too far off. My dragon sense is pulling us toward the water, I think."

"We're near a wide river."

"Hope we don't have to cross. I'm not really up for a swim this close to gator territory." My scare back in the Everglades had given me my fill. They'd been pretty friendly, but their teeth had been damned big.

I set off across the uneven ground, trying to avoid stepping over graves. Roarke followed, and we stuck to the paths whenever possible, but the most direct route was sometimes across the graves. Magic shivered on the air, something strange that I'd never felt before. It was dry and cold. Freaking creepy.

"Horrible magic," I muttered.

"Ghosts." Roarke pointed.

I peered in the direction he indicated, making out the pale gray forms of ghosts in the distance. If I strained my ears, I could hear heckling. The jeering tones were unmistakable.

"Are those ghosts chasing another ghost around a sarcophagus?" I squinted, just able to make out a man dressed in a nice suit and hat, being chased by a group of people. The group was *pissed*, if their cries were any indication.

"He must have been an asshole in life," Roarke said.

"No kidding. Made plenty of enemies."

We hurried on, skirting around the scene and leaving the angry ghosts to their vengeance. Whatever that guy had done to them in life, they wanted their piece of his hide.

A massive obelisk loomed to our right, piercing the night sky like some dead guy's version of a Ferrari or other status symbol.

"Lotta rich dudes here." The words had just left my mouth when I caught sight of a girl standing at the base of the obelisk. Her back was to us, but she wore a thin blue dress and had long braids down her back. For a moment, I thought she was a ghost. But her dark skin shook some sense into me. She wasn't nearly transparent enough to be a ghost.

Not only was her silent presence a bit creepy, but eerie magic radiated from her, a signature that I'd never felt before.

"Quickly," I whispered as I hurried by her. I didn't want to tangle with that girl. Not only was she possibly grieving—or doing weird magic—she was powerful. No need to borrow trouble.

Roarke and I hurried as silently as we could, leaving the girl behind. I was so focused on putting as much distance between myself and the girl that I missed the prickly magic that raced over my skin.

Magic crackled with energy as we stepped over an invisible tripwire.

"Shit!" My gaze skated over our surroundings.

For a second, nothing happened.

Then a low, sonorous voice echoed through the night. "Be gone."

CHAPTER TWO

"No problem," I muttered as I hurried between two massive headstones. "Sure as heck don't want to meet you."

"Be gone." The voice rumbled low again.

I hurried my pace, Roarke just behind me as we weaved in between the headstones.

"To the left." Roarke's low voice dragged my gaze in that direction.

Silvery gray forms were climbing out of the ground right in front of gravestones, their forms withered and terrifying. They were like zombies and ghosts combined, with a chilly magic that froze the blood in my veins.

But these were no zombies. They were all ghosts, and they were fast. Within seconds, a dozen had climbed out of the ground, their ravenous black gazes on us.

"These guys are bad news." I'd only ever encountered neutral or helpful ghosts. These were anything but neutral.

As Roarke shifted into his demon form, I let my Phantom magic flow through me. It glowed blue and bright in the dark night, so different than the pale gray ghosts that flowed toward us.

I drew my sword from the ether as they neared, swiping out for the nearest attacker. My blade passed right through it.

"Shit!" My blade always had an effect on Phantoms. But not the ghosts?

The creature reached for me with skeletal hands, its ragged cloak whipping about its form. Black eyes seared into me as it clutched my shoulders. Icy electricity shot from its hands, right into me.

I thrashed, trying to throw it off, but failed. The thing clung hard to me, shooting its icy electric pain through me. At my side, Roarke fought two more ghosts. He managed to throw them off, but couldn't kill them. They were wounded—moving slowly and limping—but apparently Roarke couldn't kill the dead, no matter what Underworld magic he possessed.

My ghostly attacker dragged me to the ground. Would he try to pull me through? Panic made my heart beat like a thousand drums.

"Roarke!" I cried.

Roarke threw off another ghost, sending the form flying through the air. It wouldn't stay gone for long, that was damned sure, but it gave Roarke time to yank me away from the ghost who was wrapping his horrible arms around me.

I shuddered and righted myself, stumbling away from Roarke.

"We have to run!" No way we could fight these things.

But they surrounded us, ravenous beasts that wanted to feed on…us?

I didn't know how they planned to do it, but after that one ghost's terrible embrace, I didn't want to know more.

"There are too many." A ghost flung itself at Roarke as the words left his lips.

He grimaced, then grabbed the thing and threw it off. Another lunged for me, wrapping electric arms around my waist. I thrashed and kicked, trying to heave it off of me, but it did no good. My Phantom magic was worthless with ghosts, and Roarke could only wound them, probably because he was Warden of the Underworld and dead things were his jam. But these dead things walked the earth, not the Underworld, so he couldn't kill them. Somehow they were different than the Phantoms he'd managed to dispatch—a magic that neither of us understood.

Two more ghosts lunged for me while another four went for Roarke. They were on us before we could blink, dragging us to the ground.

Fear pounded in my chest as I struggled within the ghost's electric grasp.

"Can't break their hold!" I gasped.

Roarke threw a couple off of himself, but two more came.

We were doomed. These ghosts were more powerful than any I'd ever seen, and there were so many that we stood no chance.

Electricity was coursing through me, a thousand shocks that weakened my muscles as the spirits worked their terrible magic.

"Halt!" A powerful voice flowed through the graveyard, prickling the hair at the nape of my neck. The ghosts froze, their arms still wrapped around me and sending pain racing through my limbs.

"Step away from them." The voice was feminine, I realized.

The ghosts obeyed, unwrapping their arms and drifting away from me. But their hungry black gazes stayed glued to me. Even their jaws hung open, as if they were salivating for a taste.

Roarke and I scrambled to our feet. The girl with the long braids raced toward us, her amber eyes glinting in the moonlight.

"Hurry!" she cried. "I cannot hold them for long. We must run."

She was graceful and swift, a gazelle of a girl who knew this land as well as the rabbits and squirrels that lived here. I raced after her, Roarke at my side. The pain slowed me at first, but slowly, it faded and I ran faster, barely keeping up with the girl as her blue dress whipped in the wind.

We followed our savior across the graveyard, dodging headstones and monuments, leaping over flowers and low walls. When I risked a glance over my shoulder, I caught sight of the ghosts, now unfrozen and following us across the graveyard. They were still a ways off, thank fates, so we had a chance.

I sprinted harder, panting as I chased the girl. She led us out of the graveyard and to the woods, not stopping until we were near a ramshackle house crouched between enormous oaks.

Breathing hard, I asked, "What were those things?"

The girl turned. She was pretty, probably only twenty years old, and she was barefoot.

"Haints." Her voice rolled with the southern drawl of Savannah. "Evil spirits with unfinished business. They can't leave Bonaventure. We're safe here in the woods."

"Thanks for saving us." I wanted to ask what her magic was, but didn't dare. It seemed rude, and I didn't want to mess with this girl.

She inclined her head. "You're not from around here."

"No." I stuck out a hand. "Del Bellator."

She took it, her handshake firm. "Aleta Indigo."

Roarke shifted back to human form before sticking out his hand. "Roarke Fallon."

Roarke and Aleta shook hands, then she looked at me. "You're different. You're magic... It's..." Her eyes widened. "You're Phantom. But that's not possible. You look human."

"Um..." Gee, I was handling this well.

"We're not too fond of Phantoms around here. Best you keep that to yourself."

No one was fond of Phantoms, so I wasn't surprised. But at least Aleta wasn't running off. She seemed too brave to be afraid of me anyway.

"What are you here for?" she asked.

"I'm looking for a place called Oriamor." So far, I'd seen no demons and definitely no portal, so something was up. My dragon sense was never wrong, but this smelled fishy.

"Never heard of it." Her sharp gaze darted left.

I turned to see her looking at the small house behind me. A patch of red flashed in the window.

"Oh, hell no," Aleta muttered.

I turned back to her as she took off running toward the house, her thin blue dress flapping in the wind. She was quick, reaching the house in seconds and scrambling through the open window.

"This girl is kinda nuts." I hurried after her, Roarke at my side.

"Seconded," he said as we pulled to a halt at the window.

I peered into a bedroom. A horrifying, red-skinned person crouched on the bed, looming over a prone body. It took a moment to register that the person had no skin—the bright red was their skinless form. Muscles, tendons, and arteries were all visible and blood red. Evil magic welled from the beast, smelling like rot and tasting like death.

The beast was killing that person in the bed! I didn't know how, but it was clearly stealing its life force.

Aleta stood beside the horrible scene. Her strange magic swelled on the air, a signature that I still couldn't identify. A moment later, the creature on the bed was flung off by an invisible force. It shook itself like a dog, then hurtled from the room, straight out the window.

Toward me.

I ducked, but it was too late. The monster slammed into me. Its flesh was warm and slippery and felt distinctly like raw meat. *Ugh.*

I crashed to the ground beneath it, my heart pounding. I thrashed, kicking and punching. No way this monster was going to suck the life from me. The creature's grip was insanely strong as it pulled at my arms. I'd never felt a creature so powerful. Agony raced over my body. My skin felt like it was separating from muscles where the beast pulled at me.

I shrieked as Roarke pulled it off of me. It took him several tries—the creature was as strong as he was.

As soon as I was free, I leapt up, ignoring the pain in my shoulders as I drew my sword from the ether. I lunged for the creature that Roarke held in front of him, stabbing my blade into its gut and yanking it free to swipe it across the monster's neck. The head toppled to the ground.

Panting, I stumbled back as it rolled to me.

"What the hell is that thing?" Roarke threw the body away from himself.

"No clue." Stomach churning, I dragged my gaze away from the head and looked into the house.

Aleta was bent over the person on the bed, checking on them. It was a young woman, and she looked mostly okay, though shaken up.

"Don't let de hag ride ya," Aleta murmured to the woman, who nodded. "And paint your windowsills and porch ceiling blue. Otherwise, you're asking for it."

The woman smiled wryly and nodded again, then Aleta turned and climbed back out the window.

Her gaze fell to the head at my feet. "You killed a Boo Hag."

"Yes." I avoided looking at the head. "What's a Boo Hag?"

"An evil beast. It rides a person, sucking out their life force while they sleep. Doesn't kill 'em. Not normally. But if they struggle..." She shook her head, her gaze disturbed. "It'll tear their skin right off and wear it."

Oh, hell no. It'd been trying to tear my skin off and... "Wear it?"

Aleta nodded. "During the day, yes. At night it must hang up its skin so that it can fly around and steal the energy from those who sleep."

"Great."

"At least there is one less Boo Hag," Roarke said.

"Well done," Aleta said. "It's difficult to kill a Boo Hag. Nearly impossible."

"Not for Del," Roarke said.

It was a strange compliment—that I was good at killing—but I was. So I'd take it.

"Clearly." Aleta's smile dimmed. "But I think it's time for you to get out of here. It's dangerous, especially for outsiders. Hate to see you run into the lizard man."

I grimaced. After running into the Skunk Ape, I wasn't keen on running into any more southern humanoid monsters.

"I think you're right." I called on my dragon sense. It immediately pulled me east, toward the river. "Are we close to the river?"

"Very close. What do you need there?"

"I think I need to cross it."

Doubt flashed across her face. "There's no place called Oriamor over there."

"I still need to go that way." I had to see whatever my dragon sense was pulling me toward.

Aleta's eyebrows rose as she blew out a breath. "If you must."

She gestured, then turned and walked through the woods. We followed. She might seem flighty, but she was powerful and she'd helped us and the girl in the house. It was definitely worth trusting Aleta Indigo.

Crickets chirped and the Spanish moss rustled as Aleta led us toward the river. The water glinted darkly in the moonlight as we neared. Aleta turned a sharp right, leading us down the water toward a faint gray glow. As we drew closer, I realized that we were walking toward more ghosts.

"Those aren't haints, are they?" I asked.

"No. Just regular ghosts, waiting to get across the river."

"They can't just fly across?" Roarke asked.

"Not in these parts. Ghosts can't cross water. So they wait for the ferry that'll take them to Ol' Beau's."

"What is Ol' Beau's?" Roarke asked.

"A bar. Maybe you'll find answers there. It's the only thing across the river. Just wait for the ferry and pay the ferryman what he asks. He'll see you across." She stopped about fifty yards from where the ghosts waited and gestured for us to join them.

"Thank you, Aleta," I said. "Do we owe you anything?"

Ire flashed in her eyes. "I don't help people for money."

Suddenly, I felt like a real tool. "I didn't mean that. It's just that you're really helpful. Kinda like a....Spooky Southern Superman, flying around and helping people."

She grinned, her white teeth flashing in the dark night. "I like that. Spooky Southern Superman. I'm not normally in the business of racing to everyone's aid, but I'm not going to ignore a good person in need."

"Well, thank you. You saved our lives."

"Not a problem. But now, I've got an old friend to visit." She inclined her head, then turned and sauntered off through the trees, back toward the graveyard.

"She's visiting an old friend in the graveyard?" Roarke mused.

"Fitting, for the Spooky Southern Superman."

"Fair enough."

I grinned at him, and he grinned back. Then, by silent agreement, we approached the small crowd of ghosts who waited by the shore. When we neared, I realized that they were sitting on park benches. A wooden overhang formed a rain barrier, though I wasn't entirely sure that ghosts needed to be protected from the rain. All in all, it looked exactly like any old bus stop. Except it was deep in the southern woods outside of Savannah and populated by ghosts.

We joined the ghosts, hovering slightly off to the side instead of taking a seat, and I made wary eye contact with what could only be described as a pirate. He had a long beard studded with braids and beads, a missing eye, and a peg leg. His hat was a battered leather three-sided affair, and a parrot sat on his shoulder. Beside him sat a priest, and next to them a woman in a lovely dress.

I smiled weakly at them. Only the pirate smiled back, showing his three teeth. His *only* three teeth. This guy had had a rough life before he'd died. But then, all of the eighteenth century had been rough.

It didn't take long for the ferry to puff into sight.

"Thank fates that the boat isn't a ghost," I muttered. "We'd fall right through to the water."

Roarke chuckled as the small steamboat pulled alongside the little wooden dock. Smoke billowed from its stack, disappearing into the dark night air. The little vessel was piloted by a man in a long dark cloak. We boarded behind the ghosts, stepping carefully onto the wooden deck as the boat rocked.

Up close, it was clear why the ferryman wore his cloak. He had no face. Just a black spot where his head should be. Instead of eyes, there were dull flames.

Freaking creepy.

He held out a hand, which was nothing more than his cloak draped over an invisible limb.

"How much?" I asked.

He wiggled his fingers—at least I thought they were his fingers, from the way his cloak was moving—and said nothing. I glanced back at Roarke, who shrugged.

I hadn't noticed what the other ghosts had given him. Dang it, I should have paid more attention.

"Give him some of yer soul," the pirate muttered.

My gaze darted to his. "My what?"

"Yer soul."

"No."

"He won't take much, and you got plenty." He glanced around. "Anyway, you see another boat willing to pick you up?"

He had a point. "He won't take much?"

"Just a smidgen. Hold out your palm." He gestured, indicating what I should do.

I glanced back at Roarke, who nodded. He was right. We needed to find Oriamor, and we didn't have a lot of time. Swimming was out of the question.

I held out my palm. The ferryman reached out as if he were going to pluck a pebble off my upturned palm. There was a pinch, and a sense of loss, then it was over.

Not so bad, really. Except my chest felt slightly hollow. It faded as I stepped forward, joining the pirate while Roarke paid the ferryman.

"I didn't see you do that," I muttered to the pirate.

"Got an account. Pay up front and you get a discount." He grinned, his three teeth shining in the moonlight.

"How…modern."

Roarke joined us, glancing at the pirate. "Why is this bar across the river if the price is so steep to get there? Couldn't you just build one in the graveyard?"

"Don't want to party where I live, do I?" The pirate huffed. "Never. I spend too much time in that place as it is."

"Fair enough." Though it was a steep price, considering he'd eventually disappear if he gave away too much of his soul. "There's not an, um…portal over there, is there? One spilling out demons?"

The pirate arched a bushy brow at me. "That sounds dangerous." He grinned, showing off his three teeth. "I like danger."

"That's not why you're crossing the river, though, right? There's no portal? Just a bar?"

"Not last that I saw."

"Nothing called Oriamor?" Roarke asked.

The pirate's forehead scrunched. "Oria-what?"

"I'll take that as a no." I leaned back against the railing, wondering what we'd find on the other side of this river.

The boat puffed across, cutting across the silent expanse of water as it chugged toward the other shore.

"Pretty lady!" the parrot chirped.

I frowned at the bird, then smiled. It wasn't every day I was complemented by a bird, so I'd take it. But the charm ended there. The pirate kept leering at me, and since I didn't want to start a fight with a toothless ghost *and* his parrot, I ignored him.

The boat drifted to a stop at the small dock, and we followed the ghosts onto the bank. It was identical to the other side, an abandoned expanse dotted with oaks dripping Spanish moss.

As the ghosts headed off, I called on my dragon sense. It pulled me in the same direction as the ghosts.

"I guess we follow them," I said.

"Easy enough." Roarke glanced around. "And Aleta was right. There's nothing else out here."

I kept my senses alert as we walked, but I could sense no portal. Roarke was taut as a wire beside me, but he, too, gave no indication that there was a portal here.

The trees thickened as we followed the dim lights of the ghosts. Finally, they were so big and close together that they formed a roof overhead. The Spanish moss dripped down like stalactites and fireflies fluttered in the air, giving the place an even more enchanted feeling. A hundred yards ahead, the air glowed brightly with the light of dozens of ghosts.

"It's definitely a ghost bar," I said. "And no portal."

"As long as there are no haints, I'll be good."

"Agreed."

As we neared, I could see that there were more than just ghosts here. Other species of supernaturals mingled with the crowd—weres and witches, demons and druids, but the ghosts outnumbered them by a factor of four to one. They all gathered around tables built of stumps. The bar was a long expanse of oak limbs that had been smoothed off at the top. Though there were no walls and the ceiling was made of the treetops, the place felt like a real bar. Just more outdoorsy.

"I guess we'd better get a drink and ask around," I said.

Roarke nodded and we headed to the bar. The bartender was a bulky man, with muscles on top of muscles. He looked a lot like The Rock, but with tiny little horns and two long fangs. The Rock, Vampire Edition.

He grinned toothily at us. "What'll it be?"

"Wine?" I asked.

"What box is your preferred vintage?" he asked.

I laughed. My boxes had no vintages. "You've got a knack for guessing drinks."

He shrugged, grinning. "It's my job."

"I'll take whatever you have. Red."

"Scotch. Neat," Roarke said.

The bartender was quick with our drinks. As I accepted it, I had the fleeting fear that I'd have to pay with some of my soul, but fortunately he accepted credit cards. Thank fate for small favors, because even boxed wine wasn't worth part of my soul. Though I didn't want to ever have to put that to the test.

Roarke paid and we took our drinks, turning around to survey the crowd.

"We need someone alone who looks friendly," I said.

"Not him, then?" Roarke pointed at a grumpy-looking troll who sat off to the corner. He was as big as a car and had a face that would turn you to stone if you looked at it too long.

"Maybe as a last resort." I scanned the crowd, which was mostly a crew of revelers, then pointed at a friendly old man who sat in the middle of the room, smoking a pipe and staring off into the distance. He was a ghost who looked like he'd had a good long life and was enjoying the memories. "Him?"

"Looks promising."

I turned to the bartender, then gestured to the man. "Could I have one of whatever he drinks?"

"Clyde? He likes Beastly Bourbon."

I nodded. "Beastly Bourbon, then."

The Rock, Vampire Edition, turned and poured the drink, then handed the glass to me. It glowed blue and pale—a ghost cocktail. Tentatively, I took it. The glass was unnaturally chill against my fingertips and felt insubstantial, but I was able to hold it.

I paid and glanced at Roarke. "Let's do this."

We approached the old ghost, who still stared off into space.

"Can we join you?" I asked.

He jumped, then his gaze landed on us. It was friendly enough, despite its transparent nature. "Don't see why not."

"Thanks." I set the drink down in front of him. "Bartender says you like Beastly Bourbon."

"He'd be right." He finished off the last sip in his old glass and took the new. "Mighty kind of you."

"Well, not really," I said. "We were hoping we could ask you some questions."

"Still kind. Coulda asked the questions without the drink."

"That'd just be rude." I scowled.

He cracked a smile that was decorated with as few teeth as the pirate. Dental hygiene in the past hadn't been top notch, apparently.

I sipped my wine, giving him a chance to try his bourbon. He did, smiling broadly, then asked, "What did you want to know?"

"Have you ever heard of a place called Oriamor?"

"A place? No."

My heart dropped, but then he spoke again. "But a person... Yes."

"Person?" That wasn't what the Shadows had said.

"Yep." He nodded toward the other side of the bar.

I turned to look.

"See that gal over there? The one with the tray? That's Zoya Oriamor."

"She's a waitress here?"

"Yep. Has been for decades."

"She doesn't look that old," Roarke said.

He was right. Zoya didn't look to be a day over thirty. She must be a long-lived species of supernatural.

"What is she? Fae?" I asked.

Clyde shrugged. "Don't rightly know. She's not the sharing sort. Seems like a runner to me."

"You mean she's hiding from something?" I sipped my wine.

"Exactly. And she couldn't have found a better place to do it."

I glanced around at the remote bar, hidden far out in the Georgia barrier islands. Clyde was right. Zoya had found a good place to hide out. But from what?

I stood. "Thank you, Clyde. We'll leave you to it."

He raised his glass and nodded, and we departed. It wasn't hard to track Zoya down through the crowd. Though she was small, she was one of the few solid-state supernaturals in the room. Was that what I should call the non-ghosts? I'd never had to think about it before.

We found her loading glassware onto the end of the bar, her blonde hair piled high on her head.

"Zoya Oriamor?" I said.

She turned, brushing her wispy bangs off her head. I could feel no magical signature from her, which was strange. Her eyes were a bright, piercing blue, and I had the uncomfortable sensation that she could see right into my soul. Her T-shirt was hot pink with the acronym

GRITS: Girls Raised in the South emblazoned across her chest.

"What do you want?" she drawled, chewing on a piece of gum.

"I'm Del Bellator. Could we ask you a few questions?"

She looked at me skeptically. "What could you possibly want to ask me? I don't deal in information." She hoisted a dirty beer glass. "I deal in PBR and Miller Lite."

I grinned. Cass would like her. "It'll only take a moment."

She sighed and nodded to an empty table a few feet away. "Fine. Wait for me there."

It only took her a few minutes to take care of the beer glasses, and she joined us, a beer in hand. She sat down heavily for such a small woman and sighed. "The ground may be made of moss and dirt, but it's still tough on the ol' dogs."

I grinned. "We wanted to ask you about your last name. Oriamor."

"Oriamor? My last name is Bennis, not Oriamor." Her gaze shifted left.

Something was fishy here. "Are you sure? Clyde over there said it was Oriamor."

Her gaze darted to him, and she scowled briefly. Though she wiped it off her face quickly, it was obvious.

"Clyde was right, wasn't he?" Roarke said. "That is your last name."

Zoya sighed. "Fine. It was, once. When I first arrived. I'd forgotten that old codger knew it. He's been around two hundred years and knows too much."

"So you are hiding, then, if you changed your name," I said.

"None of your business," she snapped.

"Fair enough." I shrugged. "I've spent most of my life hiding so I can understand that. And I'm not here to ask about you. I'm here to ask about a place called Oriamor."

Her skin paled, the blood rushing out of her face in a flash. She drew in a quick, quiet breath. "Doesn't exist."

"Sure it does," I said. "Your face tells me that."

"Damn it." She dragged a hand through her blonde hair. "I've gotten bad at this. Been here two centuries, safe as can be, and forgot how to keep my cool."

"I hope that's me one day—so safe I forget to be wary," I said.

Sympathy entered her eyes. "What is it you want to know about Oriamor? I left there long ago."

"I screwed up." I grimaced. "Bad. Some evil jerks forced me to open a portal between the Underworld and Earth. They said that it opened in a place called Oriamor. Because of me, there are now hundreds of demons spilling out onto Earth, right into Oriamor."

Zoya sagged in her chair. "So the legend was true."

"What legend?" Roarke asked.

"Oriamor was a settlement built by Ice Fae in Kamchatka, Russia. It's a peninsula even farther east than Siberia. Truly the back of beyond."

I pointed to her T-shirt. "So you're no GRITS, and your accent is a good fake."

She nodded sharply. "My people lived in Oriamor for thousands of years, but a shadow always hung over our head. The place was haunted by a dark magic—one that we didn't understand nor like. But it was one of the few uninhabited active volcanic areas in the world, so we chose it as our home. We like the combination of fire and ice. The Ice Fae draw their power from the earth—we need to live by an area like that to be worth anything."

"So when you left, you lost your powers," I said. And it was the reason I couldn't feel any coming off of her. "Must have been something scary to drive you away."

She nodded. "It drove all of us away—all that were left, at least. The dark magic had grown with time, causing accidents and deaths. There were only about a few dozen of us left. I escaped before it got me too. I don't know what happened to the rest of my people. I just wanted to put it behind me—live a good, simple life."

"You mentioned a legend?" Roarke asked.

Zoya nodded, her face still pale. "The Legend of the Overwhelming. It's the main reason I left. Our seers believed that the dark magic was a precursor to a great portal opening from hell. Demons would flow out, destroying our town and everyone in it."

"Overwhelming you," I said.

"Exactly. Oriamor means gateway in our language, so it made sense."

"If Oriamor means gateway, why is it your last name?" I asked.

"It also means Gatekeeper. That's me. Or rather, my family. We were the gatekeepers, protecting our village. But with the magic getting stronger and more accidents occurring, we decided the time was coming. So I left."

"But you were off by two hundred years," I said.

"Over the course of several thousand years, that's not so much. Especially for someone as old as a Fae."

"True enough," I said. "How did everyone else feel about you leaving?"

"About as you'd expect—pretty negatively. I'll never be allowed back. Killed on sight, according to the rules."

"That's a big sacrifice to make," I said.

"No kidding. But it was the right call. The prophecy has come to pass. The portal is open. The demons are coming through. I got out. I'm safe."

"What about everyone else?"

She shrugged. "Killed or they've made some pact with the demons. Either is possible. They could still be there—but they're lost to me. They have been since I broke the rules and fled."

"I'm sorry," I said.

"Don't be. I made my choice." Her voice was hard. Despite her slight stature and pretty face, I could see the tough woman who'd made the best choice for her own survival and stuck with it.

"We need you to tell us how to get there so we can close it."

She laughed, a dark, bitter sound. "Not a chance in hell, cookie. There's no way you'll ever make it close.

The place is too protected. I'd be sending you to your deaths."

"We're good at breaking through protections," Roarke said.

She shook her head. "Not good enough. Because we fight over our turf, Ice Fae have gotten good—no, *great*—at protecting their territory. You've never seen anything like what we've got in Kamchatka. We own almost the whole peninsula." She frowned. "Or at least, we did."

"Does that mean the enchantments might be defunct?" I asked. Though we probably *could* fight our way through, that didn't mean I wanted to. We needed to be fast and effective, not hampered by delays.

"Not a chance," Zoya said. "They'll be there. And you won't get through."

"Then take us through," Roarke said. "You're from the line of gatekeepers—you'd be the best at getting through the protections."

Zoya laughed. "Hell no. My people will kill me on sight if I return. And how do I even know you're telling the truth?"

"Hardly seems like something anyone would make up," I said.

She shrugged. "Takes all sorts."

"We'll pay you," Roarke said.

"I gave up my powers to escape that place. I'll never be accepted back because I ran. They might even kill me." She shook her head. "Ain't nothing you can offer that'll convince me."

I grimaced. Her tone was so determined. She had set up camp on this remote island two hundred years ago and wouldn't be leaving anytime soon.

Behind her, there was a curse and a shuffle. I peered around Zoya's shoulder. There were more people in the bar now, a cluster of raggedy looking fellows. I squinted.

Demons.

Seven of them.

Two more appeared, making a total of nine. All were laden down with weapons.

"Zoya?" I asked. "Are demons a common occurrence here?"

"Not particularly. Too far off the beaten path for their shenanigans."

Hmmm. That's what I'd been afraid of. I shared a glance with Roarke. From the glint in his eyes, he shared my concern. This wasn't the first time I'd been hunted by demons.

The newcomers were scanning the crowd, clearly searching for someone. They clustered around a big demon—easily seven and a half feet tall—who had thick horns and a bulbous nose. A large sword hung at his side.

These guys *definitely* weren't here for just a beer.

The leader's gaze landed on me and narrowed.

CHAPTER THREE

The demon who stared at me muttered something to the one next to him.

"Yep, they're looking for you," Roarke murmured.

"We shouldn't take our invisibility potions, or we'll lose our shot at convincing Zoya to take us to the Oriamor," I whispered. "Let's kill these guys and get back to convincing her."

Roarke nodded.

Zoya gazed at us with her brows raised, trying to make out our low words, then turned to look at the demons.

"Shit," she muttered. "They look like trouble."

"At least there are only nine of them." I stood, drawing my sword from the ether.

"That's a lot," Zoya muttered.

"We've faced worse." Roarke shifted into his demon form, eliciting a gasp from Zoya.

The demons charged, shoving aside tables and tossing patrons to the ground. Clyde jumped up and grabbed his bourbon, then sprinted for safety. He was spry for an old ghost.

The big boss demon led the way, but I wasn't worried about him. Not yet. It was the fire demons on either side of them who caught my eye. Each had powered up a fireball that glowed red hot in their hands.

Aleta's words about Phantoms flashed in my mind. Instead of shifting, I dodged the first fireball by inches. Zoya threw herself to the ground and crawled toward the safety of the bar. The second fireball flew for my chest. Though I lunged to the side, it grazed my shoulder in a blaze of pain.

Roarke took to the air, hurtling toward the oncoming demons. He grabbed each of the fire demons by the collar and hoisted them into the air, then tossed them into the river. They landed with a massive splash and didn't surface. Should have learned to swim.

An unconventional fire extinguisher, but it worked.

Roarke took on two more demons while I powered up an icicle and shot it at the big guy. He batted it aside, too quickly for such a large figure. Apparently he had strength *and* speed.

So I was screwed. Especially since he still had four smaller demons flanking him, and they were only a dozen yards away.

Fortunately, the pirate ghost came to my aid, taking on a smaller demon by hurling himself at him and wrapping his arms around the thin red body. The demon shrieked.

"Burn!" cried the parrot.

Flirty *and* bloodthirsty, that bird.

I tried one more time with an icicle, but the big demon batted it away. Shit. Dumb. I needed to quit going for the big guy and take out someone who couldn't throw off my defenses.

I narrowed my eyes and aimed at the demon farthest to the left, a slender gray one who carried a broad axe that I didn't want to meet the business end of. Fortunately, he wasn't so fast. The icicle hit him in the side when he was too slow to dodge, and he went down hard. Clyde ran in for a kick, not spilling a drop of his bourbon.

Roarke plucked up one of the last two small demons and carried him high into the air, breaking his neck. The big demon was close enough that I lunged for him, swiping out with my sword.

It bounced off of his rubbery hide. I tried again, this time stabbing toward his middle. It didn't pierce him—not a single inch.

He grinned at me, his yellow teeth sharpened into points.

"What the hell are you?" I demanded.

"Death," he rumbled.

"Sorry, bud, that's me." But his resistance to steel would come in handy if I could steal his power.

How, though? I'd have to shift—and that wasn't a good idea in front of all these people.

The thought was swept from my mind as he reached for me with one big hand. He was fast as a snake, grabbing me by the collar and yanking me toward him. He wrapped his beefy arms around me and squeezed.

The breath burst from me as he crushed my lungs. My ribs ground together. Blackness edged into my vision. Pain enveloped my chest as my ribs cracked.

Holy shit, he was crushing me to death. He was so fast and so strong that he'd gotten the upper hand in a heartbeat.

"The Shadows send their regards," the demon growled from behind me. His breath was hot on my ear. *Ugh.*

I glanced up, frantically searching for Roarke through blurry eyes. But he was nowhere. The blackness crept in until I could only see a pinprick. I had only seconds.

Desperately, I shifted into my Phantom form, letting the icy magic fill me. The pain lingered, but my vision cleared as the pressure of his arms no longer affected me.

"What the hell!" the demon rasped.

"Monster!" cried a ghost, pointing at me.

Fuck that guy, I had work to do. I leapt away from the demon, spinning to face him. Out of the corners of my eyes, I could see the horrified expressions on the bar patrons' faces as they looked at me.

"Phantom!" one cried. "She'll steal your soul!"

The priest who'd been on the boat over with us made a cross over his chest.

It hurt. I wasn't normally prone to caring about other's opinions, but I'd never revealed myself as another in front of so many people.

And they all thought I was a *monster.*

Fuck 'em. I shook away the concern and focused on the demon who'd almost killed me. I needed to focus—to use some kind of magic that he couldn't fight.

He stepped toward me, so I used my telekinesis to throw a wooden stump at him. He tripped over it, slowing briefly, but righted himself. I threw another stump, giving it as much juice as I could, and it hit him in the head. He wobbled, eyes rolling, and I used his distraction to throw an icicle at him.

He tried to bat it away, but the disorientation made him too slow. The thing plowed into his chest, piercing the skin and muscle. It didn't sink as deep as it normally would, but he toppled backward.

Behind him, Roarke took out the remaining two demons, quickly tearing their heads from their bodies.

I rushed forward, about to steal his power, but the gazes of the bar patrons pulled me up short. They stood in a massive circle around me, eyes riveted to my icy blue form. Fear and disgust glinted in their gazes.

Right.

Monster. That was me.

I slowed to a halt. I couldn't steal this demon's power—not in front of these guys.

"She's going to steal his soul," muttered one.

"Abomination," said another.

Shit. They had a point. I *did* steal their souls when I took their powers. Guilt crept in. I changed back to human. Roarke landed next to me and glared at everyone.

"Got a problem?" he demanded.

They all shifted uncomfortably, then broke up and drifted away, taking up their seats at the bars.

Warmth filled me, and I glanced at Roarke. "Thanks."

"Anytime."

The demon's bodies would disappear soon. I knelt by the one closest to me, rifled through his pockets, and pulled out a transportation charm. Jackpot.

"Check the others," I said.

There were only five demon bodies that hadn't yet disappeared. We didn't get any more charms, but at least we looked.

"They were from the Shadows?" Roarke asked.

"Yep."

I stood, then searched for Zoya. She leaned against the bar, staring at us. A frown spread across her face.

I approached, Roarke at my side.

"They were from the portal in Oriamor, weren't they?" Zoya asked.

"Yeah. How'd you know?"

"Demons don't often come here. Not that many. The ghosts bother them. But they risked it. To get to you."

I nodded. "They want to stop me from closing the portal. Their goal is to overrun Earth. Any demon who wants out of the Underworld can just walk through."

"Shit." Zoya dragged a hand through her hair and stared at the ground.

"You can see why we need your help," Roarke said. "It's desperate."

Zoya looked up, her blue eyes torn. "I know, damn it. I know." She heaved out a sigh. "Give me a moment."

She turned and walked to the edge of the bar, drifting into the woods. Once she was about twenty yards away, she pulled a phone out of her pocket and made a call. I couldn't hear what she was saying, but she was gesturing with her hands pretty like she was conducting an orchestra.

Finally, she hung up the phone and returned, her gaze resigned but determined. "I'll help you. But I can't do it until tomorrow night. I've got some things to settle here first."

"Settle?" I asked. "I don't plan to be gone long."

"I'm not allowed back into Oriamor. The protections are closed against me. I can probably get through them, but *probably* isn't one hundred percent."

And if she didn't get through them, she'd die. It was clear what she meant.

"Of course." I tried to gentle my voice. "Thank you for your help."

"Don't see as how I have any other choice." She shrugged. "Give me an address, and I'll meet you at six tomorrow night."

Victory. Her agreement had just improved our chances of success tenfold. I'd just have to do my best to see to it that she didn't get hurt and could come back here to live out the rest of her days in peace with the pirate, his parrot, and Clyde.

We walked into Roarke's house later that night. We'd considered going back to my place, but his was nicer. And I really wanted a shower in his sweet guest bath.

"I'm going to get cleaned up," I said.

"All right. We'll eat after."

I grinned. "Thanks. Glad you're always on top of that."

He shrugged. "I like to eat."

I gave him a quick kiss, then hurried up the stairs to the bathroom I usually used when I was here. I supposed I could use his, but I never had before, so I wanted to stick to the usual. We were closer than ever, but I still didn't feel quite comfortable just running around his house wherever I pleased. I knew he wouldn't care—it was more my thing. I'd never been in a truly serious relationship before, and with every day that passed, this was starting to feel like the real deal.

I couldn't resist spending a few extra moments in the grotto as the hot water pounded down upon me. The soaps and shampoos were lovely—about a thousand times nicer than the crap I used from the drugstore down the street. Fancy bath stuff wasn't my usual jam—I'd once gone six months using body wash for shampoo without realizing it—but Roarke's stuff was beginning to make me see the error of my ways.

No matter how hard I tried, I couldn't shake the memory of the ghosts back at the bar staring at me in horror. I counted the stones that made up the walls of the shower and tried to remember my multiplication tables, but it didn't clear my mind.

Eventually, I gave up and climbed out, scrubbing myself dry and putting on some pajamas that I'd stored in the dresser. Once I was fully dry, with my damp hair piled on top of my head, I sat on the bed and touched my comms charm.

"Cass? Nix? You there?"

"Here!" Cass's voice came first.

"How'd it go? Find anything?" Nix asked.

"Yeah. Oriamor the person, not Oriamor the place. But she'll lead us to it."

"Where's it at?" Nix asked.

"Kamchatka, in easternmost Russia."

Cass whistled. "That's remote."

"No kidding. And apparently it's protected by enchantments the likes of which we've never seen."

"Dang, that's something," Cass said.

I told them everything that Zoya had said, emphasizing the danger, then finished with, "So I think this is it. We've got to be ready to fight when we get there. There'll be no second chances."

"We'll go with you," Nix said.

"Ditto," Cass said.

My heart warmed, and I didn't bother arguing with them. I needed their help. And they'd never take no for an answer. I knew I wouldn't. "Thanks, guys. Meet us at Ancient Magic at six p.m. tomorrow."

My niggling concern over the ghosts' disgust with me lingered, poking at me to confess to my *deirfiúr*. But that was stupid. This worry was stupid. We were FireSouls. We were used to being considered monsters—

I should be tougher than caring what a bunch of ghosts thought.

But the things they'd said... *Soul stealer.* Was that really me?

"We'll see you tomorrow," Cass said before I could mention my concern. It was for the best.

"Later," Nix said.

"Bye." I hung up, then stood. My stomach growled, ready for food, and I headed downstairs. The house smelled of wood fire, and the walls were lit with warm light as I made my way through the living room.

I found Roarke in the kitchen, an array of ingredients set up before him, and classic rock on the radio. There were small bowls of veggies, cheese, and red sauce, along with two pizza crusts.

He looked up and smiled. "Build your own pizza. I thought you'd like it. It's fun."

I smiled, but I could feel that it didn't reach my eyes.

He frowned. "What's wrong?"

I headed toward the box of wine on the counter. "Nothing."

"Sure doesn't sound like nothing."

"I don't want to bother you with my dumb problems."

"You're never dumb."

"Debatable." I filled my coffee mug with the wine. "There was this time when I was sixteen and thought I could drive one hundred in a fifty-five."

He winced. "Well, besides that..."

I sighed. "It really is dumb, though."

"Tell me about it anyway."

I leaned against the counter and met his dark gaze. He was so handsome, with his dark hair and eyes and the thin sweater that draped so appealingly over his muscular chest. I couldn't believe a guy like him liked me, and that he wanted to listen to all my silly problems.

"Come on," he said.

"Fine. Back at the bar, the ghosts were horrified by me. By the fact that I'm a Phantom and can steal powers."

"And that bothers you?"

"It shouldn't." I wanted to throw my hands up in the air, but I didn't want to lose my wine, so I kept them down. "I shouldn't care what the ghosts think. I'm a FireSoul. I've spent my life hiding because people hate what I am. Why do I start caring now?"

"Maybe because they're a bit like you, in a way? Ghosts and Phantoms aren't too different. It's like being rejected by your own kind. That's hard."

I winced, but he might be onto something. Though that wasn't the whole of it. "I'm worried they might also have a point. About me being a soul stealer."

That was what was really bothering me. Not that they didn't like me—though it had sucked in the moment to realize it—but that they might have a point that I was a terrible person.

"How so?"

I stared hard into the deep red liquid in my cup. "When I steal powers, I do it by pulling out the demon's soul. And then they can't go back to the Underworld like other demons. So technically, I'm killing them forever. Poof! Gone. It's awful."

"Not really," he said. "I know what those demons are like—you only chose the worst of the worst. You worked hard to pick the ones who fed on pain and misery. You were careful. The world is better without them."

His words made me feel a tiny bit better. "But is it really up to me to be judge and jury?"

"When it saves lives, why not? You're working for the world's best interest, Del."

"You have a point. It's just…harder than I thought it would be, I guess. Up until now, I was just a mercenary with a side gig hunting down magical treasure."

"And things are different now."

"Exactly. I have a lot of power—almost too much. And it's kind of a dark power."

"But you're not a dark person."

"I hope I'm not. If I was going to be worried about soul stealing, I should have started worrying a while ago."

"No. You were trusting your instinct. Only now that things have gotten harder and there's more pressure than ever, you've started doubting yourself. It's only human."

I grinned, feeling a bit better. "I guess you're right. I'll take being human any day. And no matter how dark my power is, I can try to use it for good. I *have* to use it for good."

"You've always known that part of your journey would be choosing whether or not to be the Guardian or the Demise. You chose Guardian. And you're sticking to it."

"Of course!"

"See? You're commitment is clear. This new worry is just because of stress."

I hugged him, absorbing his warmth and strength as he wrapped his arms around me. "You're right. My *deirfiúr* and I have had a bit of a rough year. I think my nerves are shot."

I hadn't exactly been handling this transition gracefully, that was for sure. Last week I was stealing powers willy-nilly; this week I was a ball of doubts. But just admitting to my flaws made them feel easier to conquer. I hadn't wanted to be tasked with saving the world, but I didn't have any choice. So I should just get over my worry to get on with the job.

And after my spree last week, I had enough power. Now it was just up to me properly using it and outsmarting the Shadows.

Roarke squeezed me tight, then pulled back. "Ready to make a pizza?"

My stomach grumbled. "I think my stomach understands English."

"It's definitely ready for pizza."

I grinned and set my wine down next to one of the raw pizza crusts. We decorated ours separately. I spread the sauce liberally, the cheese generously, then went nuts with the veggies.

"Is that supposed to be Pond Flower?" Roarke pointed to my pizza.

"Yeah." I gazed admiringly at the dog's head that I'd shaped out of peppers and onions. "Looks just like her, doesn't it?"

"Sure, if you say so."

I threw a pepper spear at him. He pulled me in for a quick kiss, then smeared a thin stripe of sauce across my cheek. I laughed and pulled away, wiping at the sauce.

We put our pizzas in the oven, then leaned against the counters and sipped our wine as we waited. We chatted about all manner of things, and it was lovely. The kind of relationship I'd always wanted but didn't think was quite real. The stuff of romance novels, you know?

But it turned out that I might have found my own Fabio after all.

When the pizzas were done, we carried them out to the living room. Roarke quickly stoked the fire, and we set up camp on the couch.

I took a bite of my pizza. "Pretty good!"

"I hope so. You made it."

I smiled and kept eating, gazing into the crackling flames. This relationship stuff was pretty great, and I was pretty damned lucky.

We polished off our pizza at the same time and then snuggled into the couch. I was drifting on a warm cloud when Roarke spoke.

"I think you should move in."

My eyes flared wide. "What?"

"Move in. You know. Live with me. That sort of thing."

"Yeah, I get it. I just… I wasn't expecting it."

"Really? You spend several nights a week here anyway."

"That's unplanned. It's different." My heart pounded, and my mind raced. Joy and anxiety fought within me, warm and cold at once. I wanted to, but…

"I've got to think about it," I said. "I like my life. I like you too. But this is a big change. A fast one."

"Sure." His arm tightened around me, and then he pulled away. "Take all the time you need."

"Thanks."

"But in the meantime, I'm going to work on convincing you."

I grinned up at him. "Yeah? How so?"

"I think you've got an idea." He leaned down and kissed me, pressing his lips to mine and pulling me onto his lap.

I sighed and relaxed into him, wrapping my arms around his neck and pressing myself against him. He deepened the kiss, and my head swam. His tongue moved expertly against my own, sending frissons of pleasure through my body.

Whatever happened tomorrow, I knew that tonight was going to be a good night. And I was going to enjoy every minute of it.

CHAPTER FOUR

The next morning, Roarke used the Underpath he'd created a couple of weeks ago to take me to my parents' castle in Wales. Because of the time change, we arrived with the noon sun high overhead.

It still looked creepy and miserable. Everything was gray and ice covered. The stones were even slightly dingy, though there was nothing here but fresh air and snow to dirty them.

"What a miserable place," I muttered.

"It lacks a certain charm, that's for sure." Roarke gazed around. "Though it's impressive."

He was right. It was huge and well defended. A lot of the stonework was ornately carved, but the dismal air that hung over the place made it hard to appreciate the artistry.

"I wish Pond Flower were here," I said. "She'd really brighten the place up."

"Or make yellow snow."

I laughed. He was such a dude.

A moment later, magic shimmered on the air, and Pond Flower appeared in the middle of the courtyard. Her head swung to and fro, ears flapping, until her gaze landed on me and brightened.

"Pond Flower!" I ran for her.

She hurtled toward me, ears flapping and tongue lolling. When she reached up, she wrapped her front legs around me. At least, she tried to. It was awkward, but I hugged her back, holding her heavy body against my own. Her fur smelled like brimstone and her breath like dead bodies, but I didn't mind.

After a moment, she dropped down, then trotted over to greet Roarke.

He crouched down and scratched her head, then looked up at me. "She must have heard you."

"Yeah." I smiled. "We've always had a connection. And she really brightens this place up."

It still had a loooong way to go, but it was more cheerful with Pond Flower doing circles around the courtyard.

We headed inside, Pond Flower at our heels. The interior of the main hall was as dreary as I remembered. It was cold and gray—the floors, the walls, the chandeliers. The only color was from the paintings on the wall, but even they weren't very bright. Though the place was beautiful with its ornate floor and glittering light fixtures, it wasn't a home. It felt like a half-dead museum.

Pond Flower ran circles around the football-field-sized foyer, skidding out on the slick tiles. I smiled. We headed toward the back of the hall and down the wide stone staircase that led to the throne room in the basement. The portal that I'd partially closed a couple days ago was still there, and I was hoping to practice my skills by finishing the job.

The throne room was still sparkling and clean from Connor's handiwork, but it was as cold as ever.

"My parents clearly wanted to scare the shit out of their subjects and make it clear who was boss," I said.

"This room does the job."

We walked toward the thrones, Pond Flower at our side. Her nails clicked on the stone floor. When we reached the midpoint, I could just barely feel the change in the air.

"You feel that?" I said.

"Yeah."

"This was the part of the room that stopped Cass and Nix when we came here the first time."

"The invisible barrier that only let you and me through."

"Exactly. I think it's part of the portal. Like the magic was spreading."

"Could be."

"Well, I'm going to try to get rid of it." I cracked my knuckles and headed to the back corner where the portal was located. I hadn't noticed it on my first visit—probably because my portal magic hadn't been activated yet. But now I could sense it. And if I focused on my new talent, I could even see it.

It was a tear in the ether, like fabric sliced through the middle. It was smaller than it had been, thanks to my first attempt. But I hadn't been able to finish the drill.

I turned back to Roarke and Pond Flower. "Give me a bit of space, okay?"

"No problem."

Pond Flower hopped up onto one of my parents' thrones and curled up. She didn't really fit, but it was a cute attempt. I turned back to the portal and sucked in a deep breath.

I cleared my mind and envisioned my goal—magically sewing the portal back together. No demon was ever going to walk into my family's house again. I didn't care if they had been invited. I was officially rescinding their welcome.

My magic flowed through me, strange and foreign. I'd only used it a couple times—against my will to open the Oriamor portal and then to try to close this portal. It still felt foreign. Almost wobbly—like I couldn't get a good grip on it.

I pushed it harder, trying to command it to do my will. I fed it to the portal, begging the magic to stitch the ether back together.

Sweat rolled down my spine as I tried. The edges of the ether began to glow, like they were starting to mend. But after a while, nothing happened. My muscles trembled, and my magic fizzled. I couldn't keep ahold of it. No matter how hard I tried, it kept retreating back inside me.

"Damn it!" I stepped back, frustration beating inside my chest.

The air around the portal shimmered, magic vibrating strongly enough that I could feel it. I peered at it. I wasn't making that happen.

"What the hell? Do you feel that, Roarke?"

"I do. No idea what it is, though."

The magic continued to vibrate, and the air shimmered with a silvery gleam. A moment later, a hazy figure appeared, climbing through the portal. I drew my ice magic to the surface, charging up an icicle in case the figure was a threat.

Actually, duh, of course it was a threat—it came from the Underworld.

When my mother straightened in front of the portal, I almost swallowed my tongue. What the hell should I do now?

I stutter-stepped backward.

Her gaze focused, and she looked at me. "Delphine."

"Mother?"

"Yes." Her gaze wasn't as cold as I remembered, and slightly unsure. That was weird. Her hair was still jet black and piled in intricate coils on top of her head. Her gown was a deep cobalt blue that complimented her eyes. I hadn't realized how similar we looked until just now.

"What are you doing here?"

"I felt you trying to close the portal."

"So you came to stop me?"

She shook her head. "To help you."

"What? I thought this portal was your idea."

"I was wrong."

"You're only just now realizing that?" What the hell was going on? All the memories I had of my mother— she was a stone-cold bitch who was using me in a plot to end the world.

But now….she was different. And it was weird.

Roarke stepped up beside me and took my hand. I felt Pond Flower's head press against my hip. Warmth curled in my chest.

"Yes," she said. "It's taken death, and time away from this place, to make me realize that I was wrong. To realize that opening the portal through Oriamor was the wrong thing to do."

"No kidding. You were trying to bring about the end of the world. And you were using me to do it."

She winced. Despite that show of weakness, she still looked like one tough bitch.

My heart ached. Before I'd regained my memory, I'd dreamed of a mother who loved me. But this woman didn't love me. She never had.

"How am I supposed to believe you regret what you did? And why should I care? You're dead. And you've been dead to me since you gave me to the Monster."

"I'm sorry." She reached out toward me.

I glared at her, and she lowered her hand.

"I can understand why you don't trust me. And I'm not trying to make excuses. But I'd like to explain—at least a little. It'll help you understand this place." She gestured to the throne room. "And it'll help you close the portal."

"Fine. Start talking." The words were harsh, but I was feeling so conflicted.

"The portal was put here during my father's time. He made a pact with the demons. It was always part of my life. But it wasn't until I died and left this place that I realized the dark magic that polluted the castle. It's been ten years since my death, and in that time, I've tried to learn what was wrong with this place."

"And?"

"I think that the portal gives off a dark power that warps the castle, and those inside it. Like the evil magic from hell seeped out and polluted this place. It influenced those of us inside." She held out her hands, palms up. "Not that I'm making excuses for myself. I never should have done what I did. But this place... It warps a person."

I wanted to believe her. It wouldn't make any of it better—all of it *had* happened, and I still struggled with those memories. But it made it easier to think that something else had influenced her. No one wanted to think their mom had been horrible to them without a reason.

"So if I close the portal, this dark spell will disappear?" I asked.

"I think so."

"And you'll go back to the Underworld? This isn't an escape attempt?" I had literally no idea how I'd deal with that. No matter what she'd done to me, I wasn't up for fighting my own mother. That was simply never going to happen. And I didn't want Roarke to have to fight her either. If she didn't go peacefully, this was a no-win, shit situation.

But wasn't that my specialty? Getting out of no-win, shit situations? I sure hoped I could pull it off this time.

"Yes. I'll go," she said. "I still need to convince your father of what I believe. But if you can close the portal and remove the dark magic from this place, it will prove me right."

Since this place was like the Addams' family mansion without any of the charm, I was super invested in getting rid of the dark magic that apparently bespelled the place. More importantly, I desperately needed to master my new portal magic. Because if I couldn't do that, it wouldn't matter what shape this place was in. The world would be overrun with demons.

"And you're going to help me close it?" I asked her.

"I'll do my best. My family had a small amount of portal magic. Nothing like yours." She studied me. "But you don't want this power, do you?"

"Of course not. It's horrible. I let hundreds of demons onto Earth. Even more are coming."

"And you have to fix that. It's because you don't want the power that your mind is rejecting it. Your subconscious isn't letting you work with it."

Hmm. It made sense, in a way. I felt like I couldn't get ahold of it properly—like the magic slipped out of my grasp. "But how can I force myself to want something?"

"You need to reframe it in your mind. This is a power for good now—you will use it to fix what was broken. You, Delphine, were all the good that was in me. Now you need to turn that good toward making your power a positive force."

Tears pricked my eyes, but I blinked them back. I didn't have time for sentimentality.

"You must want your gift—embrace it," she said. "Envision it as a light that you can manipulate. A golden light that will help you."

That was how I usually thought of my magic when I was practicing something new—had I inherited that trick from her? But I hadn't used that method with this new magic—probably because I didn't truly want this new gift.

My subconscious was a tricky beast.

"Fine," I said. "I'll try it."

"You can do it, Delphine." Sincerity shone in her eyes. I felt like a kid about to attempt a penalty at my soccer game. She really believed in me and wanted me to succeed. At something important. Something good.

"I'll try." I swallowed hard, wondering what else I should tell her.

When she started to approach, I stiffened. She wasn't far away, but she was moving slowly. As if she didn't want to startle me. Smart. The slightest breeze would make me jump right now.

She stopped in front of me.

"What do you—?"

Her hug cut me off. I stiffened. She was warm and soft despite her ghostly nature. Was I imagining that? Tentatively, I let go of Roarke's hand and hugged her back. I forced the tears away by thinking of all that I had to fight ahead of me.

When she released me and stepped back, love shined in her eyes. It was weird and unfamiliar, but it made me smile.

"I'm leaving now." She turned and went to the portal. As she neared it, she looked back. "I love you, Del."

My throat tightened. As she stepped through the portal, I managed to croak out the words, "I love you too."

She hesitated just briefly, then disappeared.

"Whew." I sagged against Roarke. "That was a trip."

"No kidding." He wrapped an arm around my shoulder and squeezed. "But do you think her advice will help?"

"I'm thinking it will." More than that, I was absolutely convinced of it.

"Then give it another go." He released me and stepped back. Pond Flower followed him.

I approached the portal by a couple feet, focusing on it. This time when I called upon my magic, I tried to really want it. I imagined all the good that I would do with it, forcing the bad to the back of my mind. It hadn't been my will that had opened the portal at Oriamor. But it was my will now that would close it.

I used my old trick that my mother had suggested and envisioned my magic as a golden ball of glowing light. It was tricky at first, but eventually the light solidified inside of me. Warmth glowed inside my chest.

I sighed, relieved. *This* felt so normal. I should have realized. Instead, I'd been so wrapped up in my misery over opening the portal that I'd focused on the bad instead of the good. But there *was* good that I could do with this magic.

I directed my power toward the portal, envisioning it closing back together. It slowly stitched itself back up, growing smaller and smaller. Sweat rolled down my spine as I forced my magic toward it.

It took ages, sapping my energy and my magic.

"Take a break, Del!" Worry echoed in Roarke's voice.

"No," I rasped. It was over half finished. I could *do* this. I had to do this.

Magic was like a muscle. I needed to work out to make it stronger. This portal was nothing compared to the portal at Oriamor. That one was strong enough to let thousands of demons through. If I couldn't close this portal, I'd never stand a chance there.

I swayed on my feet, but never let my magic slow down. Finally, as my vision was beginning to blur, the portal closed.

The air changed immediately, some of the chill dissipating. As I collapsed to my knees, I realized that the whole place felt different. The dark aura that had covered the castle was gone.

I blinked. Roarke appeared in front of me, helping me rise.

"My mother was right," I murmured. "This place feels different."

"Looks different, too." Roarke gestured to the walls.

I blinked my eyes to clear them and realized that the glowing walls made of Catalight stone were even brighter. Pond Flower ran in circles, her eyes gleaming with excitement and her tongue lolling.

"Let's go look upstairs," I said.

We climbed the stairs, slowly because of my exhaustion, but even this part of the house was different. It felt lighter and warmer. More like a house instead of the haunted mansion.

But it was the foyer that shocked the hell out of me. I gasped at the sight of the colorful room. No longer done in tones of black, gray, and white, the stone floor was a kaleidoscope of color. Orange, red, and yellow stone gleamed in the light of the chandeliers, which no longer dripped ice. The walls were actually paneled in blue silk, and the paintings were even brighter than they had been. Even the glass windows had mended themselves.

"Wow." I spun in a circle, taking in the place. "This is amazing."

"You really could turn it into a ski resort now."

I laughed, remembering when I'd joked about that. I hadn't been serious—obviously no one would come to this hell hole for vacation—but now it was actually nice.

"My mother was right." I walked toward the main doors, Roarke at my side as Pond Flower led the way. "This place really was under a dark spell."

"And her with it," Roarke said.

"I guess so." I remembered what Draka had said, about my mother and father being irredeemable. Either she'd been wrong—she wasn't a god, after all—or perhaps they'd been slightly bad to begin with. Bad enough that they'd quickly fallen prey to this place's dark magic.

Either way, my mother had seen the error of her ways, and I was going to hold on to that. She'd apologized and come to help me. I had no idea how long it would have taken me to figure out the key to my new portal magic—if I ever would have.

Outside, the courtyard was no longer covered in ice, and the stone was far less dingy. I had the feeling that in the summer, this place might even have ivy growing on the walls.

Roarke and I checked out the rest of the castle. The library was even more amazing than before, colorful and bright, while the kitchens didn't look nearly as dingy and dark.

"Removing the dark magic was like the quickest cleaning spell ever," I said.

"It made a world of difference."

"Though I can't say I'm keen to move in anytime soon."

Roarke arched a brow and glanced at me. "Keen to move in anywhere else?"

I grinned. "Don't be pushy."

But my heart warmed at the idea that he wanted to live with me. That was a huge step—and an awesome one.

But it was a step I would have to think about another time. I didn't exactly have the brain power right now to decide on future living arrangements.

Roarke and I left the castle through the Underpath that he'd created. Pond Flower followed, crossing the Underpath on her own. Another talent of a hellhound.

When we arrived back in Magic's Bend, it was late afternoon. Pond Flower promptly watered a bush planted near the sidewalk. The sun was low in the sky and the air chilly. Fat gray clouds obscured the setting sun.

I tugged my jacket more tightly around me. "I think I need a coffee with a boost. I'm still dragging."

"What you need is an eight-hour nap, after all the magic you used."

"I don't think I'm going to get one."

We headed down the street toward P & P, Pond Flower at our heels.

Connor looked up as the bell on the door tinkled. He smiled, shoving his floppy dark hair out of his eyes. "Hey, guys!"

"Can Pond Flower come in?" I asked.

"Anytime." Connor waved us in. "I'll get her a bowl of water and a treat."

"She doesn't eat food."

"Right. Hellhound. Well, I'll scratch her ears, then."

"That, she'll like." I glanced around at the empty space. Pre-dinner lull. "Could I get a coffee with about a thousand boosts of energy?"

"That'll kill you." Connor shook his head. "How about three boosts?"

"I'll take it." I picked one of the few stools at the bar.

"I'll have the same, please." Roarke sat beside me. Pond Flower stretched out on the floor.

"Coming right up!" Connor got to work on the fancy espresso machine behind the bar. "Along with a couple slices of quiche of the day, okay?"

I grinned. "Perfect."

It didn't take long for Connor to whip up our drinks and our plates, and it took even less time for me to chow down.

"Whoa, breathe!" Connor's dark brows jumped up. "You're going to choke."

I swallowed. "Don't need to breathe."

"Pretty sure you're wrong on that." Connor fiddled with the dials on the stereo in the corner and pumped up the music. If I had to guess, the band was the same as the one emblazoned across his T-shirt—Alien Panda Jury. He returned to us and crouched down to pet Pond Flower, who rolled onto her back, big feet straight up in the air.

I polished off my quiche and coffee without choking to death—victory!—then glanced at the clock behind the bar. "Almost time to meet the rest of the gang."

Roarke took the last sip of his coffee and stood. "Let's get a move on, then."

I stood, feeling vastly better than I had when I'd entered P & P. We paid Connor and left, Pond Flower following along. She'd never stuck by my side quite like this before. It was unusual, but I liked it.

"Be safe!" Connor called. "Call if you need backup."

"Will do!" I waved and walked out into the chill.

"I'm going to get my bag from my car," Roarke said.

Given that it might take a while to get through the protections at Oriamor, we'd all been instructed to pack a change of clothes. Nix could always conjure things, but it was better to save her magic for the truly necessary.

"I'll grab mine from my apartment. Meet you in Ancient Magic?"

He nodded and set off. Pond Flower stuck with me as I stopped by my apartment to grab the small overnight bag that I'd packed, along with a change of lucky charms. I still wore the bracelet that Roarke had given me, but I wanted to suit up with a more varied arsenal. This was the biggest fight of my life. I couldn't afford to lose.

I met Roarke at Ancient Magic just as Nix was closing up the till, which was crowded between a giant vase and a statue of a dog. Other artifacts sat neatly on shelves, little pieces of history waiting to be taken home. Most people didn't care that they were replicas—they were only interested in the magic they contained.

"Zoya should be here any minute," I said as I swung my bag up onto the counter. Pond Flower thumped her butt onto the ground and smiled up at Nix, tongue lolling out of her mouth.

"Good. I'm already packed." Nix pulled a backpack from behind the counter. "How did it go in Wales?"

Warmth filled my chest at the memory of the castle looking so inviting. "Really well. It was hard, but I managed to close the portal. With my mother's help."

Nix's jaw dropped.

"You trying to catch flies?" I asked.

"How? That's crazy."

I told her about my mother coming out of the portal and her change of heart. It felt surreal just to think of it—the event had turned everything upside down in my head.

"How do you feel about all that?" Nix asked. Concern shadowed her green eyes.

"I honestly have no idea. Happy. Confused. Sad, for what might have been."

"Yeah, it's going to take time to process all that." She glanced at Roarke, something lighting in her eyes. "Could you possibly visit her in the Underworld? You know, now that you've got an in with the boss man?"

Something fluttered around my heart. Hope? I looked at Roarke. "Is that possible?"

He rubbed his chin, thoughtful. "If we can find her, perhaps. But you'd have to have an idea about what afterworld she might have gone to."

"Hmm..." I thought back to my youth—what I remembered, at least. Religion hadn't been big in our household. At least, not in my memories. Normally you went to whatever Underworld your religion believed in, but I wasn't sure what my parents had believed. "Maybe we'll find clues in my house. Or my dragon sense could help."

Roarke reached for my hand and squeezed. "I'll help however I can."

"That's another adventure for another time," I said. But I couldn't help but think about how much it meant that Roarke would help me find my mom. Why would I *not* want to live with this guy? He was amazing. Nix smiled at him, approval in her gaze.

Of course. She and Cass were the reason I didn't want to move away from here. We had a really nice setup, and I'd never been particularly fond of change. And though Cass was around less these days, considering the time she spent with Aidan, she was still around a lot. I couldn't think about it now.

Pond Flower jerked, spinning her head to face the door. Her ears perked up.

"What's she looking at?" Nix asked.

I squinted out the big glass windows, but saw only the park on the other side of the line of cars parked on the street.

"No idea, but—"

Pond Flower jumped up and charged out the door, cutting me off.

"I'll see what she's up to." I raced after her, shouting, "Watch out for cars!"

There were no cars to hit Pond Flower as she ran across the street. The evening sun was setting, casting long shadows across the pavement. Pond Flower raced into the park, to a cluster of bushes in the center.

I followed, unable to see what she was after. Maybe she just wanted to play. Who knew with hellhounds?

I slowed to a stop, about to turn back around and leave her to her games. A half second later, six demons popped out of the bushes. They were the size of children, but as they leapt from their hiding places, they grew into full-sized men.

"What the hell are you?" I demanded as I pulled my sword from the ether.

I'd never seen demons of their type before. They were as large as Roarke, each covered in rippling muscles and weapons of all sorts. Short horns protruded from their heads, and massive fangs hung down over their jaws. Magic had made them small enough to hide amongst the bushes.

Shame they hadn't stayed that small.

As one, they drew their swords and surrounded me. I charged up an icicle and hurled it at the nearest demon. He deflected it, quick as a snake.

Damn it.

Cold magic flowed through me as I adopted my Phantom form. Pond Flower barked, her eyes blazing red as she surrounded herself in her protective black flame and crouched in front of me, ready to jump at the first demon who approached.

I didn't wait. I lunged at the nearest one, turning corporeal long enough to stab my blade through his gut. Unfortunately, he was fast too. His steel sliced at my arm. Pain flared as I adopted my Phantom form again, just in time to save my arm from being severed.

The other demons closed in, but their weapons could hurt me in this form. I floated through the one in front of me, shuddering at the feeling of passing through another living being. As I turned to face my enemy again, I caught sight of Roarke shifting as he ran. The swirl of black smoke obscured him briefly before he burst forth, all rippling muscle and dark wings.

He was at my side a moment later, reaching for a demon while nimbly avoiding its blade. In a flash, he broke its neck.

Nix, racing behind Roarke, conjured her bow and fired at one of the huge demons closest to her. The arrow plunged into its eye socket, and the beast crashed to its back. I danced away from one who charged, not wanting to feel it pass through me, and became solid long enough to slice my blade across its throat.

Unfortunately, I wasn't quick enough to return to my Phantom form, and blood sprayed across my face. I gagged, hating the wet warmth dripping down my cheek.

Four demons down, two to go. In the distance, Aidan and Cass's Range Rover pulled up. They were too late to join the fun. Nix's arrow sank into a demon's throat just as he was about to grab her, and Roarke raced for the last demon standing.

"Wait!" I cried, shoving him aside.

He glanced at me as if I were crazy. The demon charged, blade held high. I shot a bolt of ice at the shining steal. It knocked the sword from the demon's hand, and the thing flew end over end. The demon shifted to stare at it, shock on his face.

I picked up speed and adopted my human form just in time to tackle him to the ground. His surprise over losing his blade gave the slight advantage I needed. He went down like a lead weight.

Scrambling, I straddled him and pressed my blade to his throat. He reached for me with clawed hands. Before he could grab me, one of Nix's arrows sliced through his wrist, pinning it to the ground. Roarke stepped on the other arm, restraining it.

The demon growled and spat at me. I saw it coming and dodged just in time. Demon blood was enough for me, thanks.

He stank of dark magic, the kind of rotten smell that came from doing the most evil deeds.

"Who sent you?" I demanded.

He growled again.

"It was the Shadows, wasn't it? You came through the portal?"

He snarled.

"I'll take that as a yes." I pressed the blade hard against his throat. "How did you find me? And use your words this time, or I'll take your soul and your power."

Fear glinted in his eyes, making me feel a bit like shit. I *knew* he was the darkest of evils. I could smell it on him. But his fear of me—of what I could do to him—still made my stomach turn.

"Tell me and I'll just kill you. You'll wake up in your Underworld and have a second chance," I said. No matter what, I'd do it. From the smell of him, I really didn't want his magic. I was getting sick of taking from these lowlifes.

"I don't know how they found you," he rasped. "They've got some kind of connection to you. Something magic."

Probably a result of the mind magic they'd put on me last time I'd seen them. Great.

"Are the Shadows out of hell?"

He grinned and nodded, revealing even more fangs. These ones were tiny and hidden behind his lips, but I wouldn't want them tearing into my flesh.

"Where are—"

Cunning glinted in his eyes as he lunged up and pierced his neck on my blade. He used the last of his strength to thrash, tearing through all the arteries in his neck. Before I could even consider taking his soul in retribution—which to be honest, I wouldn't have—he had bled out onto the ground beneath me.

"Well, that was quick thinking on his part," Nix said.

"And quick action." Roarke removed his foot from the demon's arm.

"If he'd answered too many questions, the Shadows might not have taken him into their employ. As it is, if he's quick, he can regenerate in hell and make it to the portal in time to get through to Oriamor."

"We'll just have to beat him to the portal, then," Roarke said. "Close it before the bastard can get out."

"I like that plan," Nix said as I patted down the pockets of the demon, looking for a transportation charm. I found none, unfortunately.

"Did we miss all the fun?"

I glanced up to see Cass grinning at me from about ten yards away. She and Aidan strolled across the park, hand in hand. The carnage around us was beginning to disappear as the demon bodies returned to the Underworld.

I was damned glad this had happened in Magic's Bend and not a human city.

I stood and dusted the grass off my knees. "Thanks for coming."

"Anytime," Cass said. "Is it about time to go?"

"Yeah. Though we should be on the lookout for more demons. They could pop up at any time."

Cass grinned. "So it'll be a challenge."

"Probably." The five of us walked back to Ancient Magic.

A woman leaned against a light pole, watching us. As I neared, I realized it was Zoya. Her gaze was shadowed and worried, her hair a mess from a long day of travel.

There was a backpack slung over her shoulder, and her jacket was of the sporty, waterproof variety.

She raised a brow and nodded at the space where the demon bodies were disappearing. "So the fun's already started?"

"It never ends," I said.

CHAPTER FIVE

Since Zoya refused to travel by Underpath or transport charm, we planned on taking Aidan's private jet. It was night and we all needed to sleep, so it would kill two birds with one stone.

We piled into Roarke's Tesla and Aidan's Range Rover and headed to the airport. We pulled away from the curb, and I gazed out the window at my motorcycle, wishing I could take that and feel the wind in my hair. But as much as I loved Scooter, he wasn't really a people mover. And with demons on my tail, it was safer to stick together.

Also, Pond Flower hadn't left my side. I'd seen little dogs in the baskets tied to bike handles before, but Pond Flower sure wouldn't fit. She squeezed into the cargo trunk of Aidan's SUV just fine though, her head resting on the seatback near my face and her stinky breath wafting past my nose.

City traffic was quiet as we drove to the airport. It took a while to remember that it was a Sunday—I was losing all track of days.

"Swanky," Zoya murmured as we pulled up onto the tarmac beside Aidan's jet. It was sleek and shiny white, but looked like any old plane to me. I loved the convenience of avoiding airport lines, but cars and planes and the like had never been my thing.

We climbed out of the vehicles. The sun had set fully, but bright stadium lights illuminated the tarmac. Roarke's assistant, a dark-haired man I'd seen a few times before, took the car keys and led us onto the plane. Pond Flower charged up the narrow metal stairs, no doubt remembering her first ride in this plane.

"Your dog likes flying," Zoya said.

"Yeah, she's a fan." After we'd rescued her from a castle in Transylvania, we'd made our getaway in this thing.

The plane was done in soft cream leather and lit with low light. Big, comfy seats filled the first half with a couple of couches in the back. There was a bedroom at the back of the plane. It wasn't the worst way to travel.

I preferred the speed of Roarke's Underpaths, but if I had to be on a plane, I wanted it to be this one. We sat in the plush seats, me next to Roarke on one side and my friends scattered around. Pond Flower stretched out in the back in the wide aisle between the two couches.

The flight attendant got us drinks as we waited for takeoff. In no time, we were in the air and speeding toward far eastern Russia. Once we were settled and had eaten a dinner of sandwiches and chips, I leaned over and tapped Zoya on the shoulder. She sat on the other side of the aisle just ahead of me.

"So, what can we expect from this adventure?" I asked.

Everyone turned to listen.

Zoya leaned into the wide aisle and turned around to look at us. "It'll take a day or two to reach Oriamor. I have a place we can bunk overnight, and a friend will meet us there, but it's going to be rustic."

"We're used to that," Nix said.

"What kind of traps and challenges can we expect?" Roarke asked.

"There are many," Zoya said. "And they are ever changing. It's been a couple hundred years since I left. We use the elements to help protect our city, and the land and the animals. We'll just have to be ready for anything."

"But you'll know the kinds of things to look for?" I asked.

"Yeah. I helped design the booby traps to catch trespassers. Things might have changed. They'll be in different locations, that sort of thing. But the premise for avoiding them will remain the same."

"You're our best shot no matter what," I said. "Thank you for coming."

Zoya grinned wryly. "I didn't really have a choice."

"Everyone has a choice."

She shrugged, then shifted back to sit in her seat. "I'm going to get some sleep. It's going to be pretty intense when we get there."

"Good idea," Cass said. "I'll hit the hay too."

She and Aidan stood, then went to the back of the plane where there was a small bedroom. Nix headed to one of the long couches, and Zoya followed her, taking the other. Pond Flower wouldn't budge, so they had to climb over her massive body.

I turned to Roarke as the lights in the plane dimmed to darkness.

"You think we can do this?" I asked.

"I do." He reached for my hand and squeezed.

"Me too." And I really did—though I liked hearing him say it. "But I'm worried about my friends. This was my fault, and now we're risking our lives. I hate putting them in danger."

"I haven't known you long, but it seems that you're always risking your lives."

I grinned. "Fair enough."

"And your friends want to have your back."

"Well, that's true." I reclined my seat, pushing the worry to the back of my mind. We'd faced a lot of dangerous things. This was just one more.

But somehow, it felt so much bigger.

Either way, we'd face it. We had to.

Roarke reclined his seat too. The things went back really far, creating a comfortable sleeping space. I curled onto my side and put my head on Roarke's shoulder. The low roar of the plane's engines lulled me to sleep as I imagined what was to come. The visions followed me into my dreams—monsters and mayhem and fire and ice. I didn't know what to expect from Kamchatka, but it couldn't be as bad as my imagination.

Could it?

The rumbling of the landing gear woke me. I snapped my mouth shut and jerked upright, surreptitiously wiping my cheek. Out of the corner of my eye, I glanced at Roarke.

No wet spot on his shoulder. Whew.

He sat up more slowly, not having freaked himself out upon waking.

"That was a comfortable night," he said.

"Anywhere with you, babe." I was only kinda joking. And when he smiled, I realized that I actually wasn't joking at all.

The lights turned on in the cabin, and Aidan and Cass came out of the bedroom, bright-eyed and bushy-tailed. Nix sat up from her couch, her hair like a rooster's. Zoya was already up and staring out the window like a kid at Christmas. She'd left this place willingly, but it seemed that hadn't kept her from missing it.

"What are our odds of getting a cup of coffee?" I asked.

"High," Aidan said. "As soon as we touch down, we'll get to-go cups."

A moment later, the plane touched down and rumbled along the runway. I found the bathroom and brushed my teeth quickly, then gave up the coveted space to the rest of the gang.

By the time I made my way back into the main cabin, the door was opening and the flight attendant was handing out coffees in to-go cups along with big muffins. My stomach grumbled as I took one.

"Thank you."

He smiled and nodded, then passed on to help the others. I was the first to climb down the stairs, Pond Flower at my side, and the icy air shocked the breath from my lungs. The airport was a low, cement building that looked like it had been built during the Cold War. To complete the picture, massive old military vehicles sat waiting for us. They were wide and low and painted a dull dark gray.

"Holdovers from the cold war," Zoya said from behind me. "Petropavlovsk-Kamchatsky is a half-human, half-supernatural town. Though the humans know nothing about the magic, of course. But this place was only accessible to military personnel during the Cold War. No civilians allowed."

"Why?" I stepped down, my eyes still on the vehicles.

"Close enough to eavesdrop on America during the Cold War. Or so they say."

I shuddered, glad that the specter of nuclear war no longer loomed. Though supernaturals were strong, we weren't stronger than nukes and human fear.

Roarke's demon staff climbed out of the two vehicles. Zoya didn't have any contacts in the human city, but Roarke did. He'd arranged transportation to get us inland to the interior where Oriamor was located. From there, Zoya would take over.

A tall demon who looked like a Russian bad guy from an action film approached. He was broad shouldered and blond, with tiny horns peeking out of his hair.

He greeted Roarke with a nod. "Boss."

"Aleks." Roarke shook his hand. "Thank you for meeting us here."

"Always." He gestured to the demon behind him. They could have been identical twins. "We are always glad for the opportunity to prove our gratitude for being allowed to live on Earth."

The others nodded.

"We will drive you," Aleks said. "Just tell us the way."

Roarke gestured to Zoya. "Follow her instructions."

We climbed up into the old vehicles. They were massively wide, with hardy old interiors that smelled of cigar smoke. Zoya rode up front to direct the driver. In the back, there were two wide benches that faced each other. Pond Flower and I sat next to Roarke, with the other three across from us.

"I feel like I've gone back in time," Cass whispered.

"There are a lot of these vehicles still on the road," Roarke said. "Though this part of Russia is now more mining and ship repair than a military outpost."

"I think I prefer mining and ship repair." My gaze was glued to the scenery outside. Tall, white-capped mountains loomed behind the city of low cement buildings. The construction was a bit dreary, but we passed by a colorful farmers' market and a lot of smiling people, so it wasn't all bad. Cyrillic writing covered all the signs, completely indecipherable to me.

Zoya led the driver out of town, through some scattered suburbs of dark wooden houses, and onto a quiet road. Small silver birches dotted the land around us.

"There aren't many roads," Zoya explained. "We'll go as far as we can, but then we'll need to take the snowmobiles that Roarke has arranged for us."

Nix perked up. "Snowmobiles?"

"Yes," Zoya said. "My people live deep inside the peninsula, within the volcanoes." She pointed to the tall mountains around us. They were volcanoes?

"The whole inland area of Kamchatka is lightly populated," she said. "About a hundred years ago, we convinced the humans to reserve this area as a national park to protect the wildlife. But our real reasoning is that Oriamor's natural defenses are so dangerous that people shouldn't be allowed to wander free. To discourage that, and because the terrain is so volatile, there aren't roads, and helicopters are a terrible idea. They'd shoot us out of the sky in no time."

"Snowmobiles it is!" Nix said. "I like them, anyway."

I didn't want to know what kind of magic could shoot a helicopter out of the sky, and I didn't want to find out.

After about an hour and a half of bouncing along on the increasingly poor road, we pulled up to a small building at the edge of the woods. It was low and wooden, crouching on the edge of an open expanse of snowy tundra.

We piled out of the vehicle, grabbing our backpacks and slinging them over our backs as a big, dark-haired man came out of the building. He smiled and greeted Roarke with a friendly handshake.

"Took you long enough to visit us out here," he said in a thick Russian accent.

Roarke grinned. "I should come back for the fishing, Igor."

Igor barked a laugh. "As if you'd ever take a vacation."

Roarke on vacation? I supposed the idea did seem a bit ridiculous. Though I kind of wanted to try it. But somewhere warmer. Here, it couldn't be more than twenty degrees, and the icy wind cut through my jacket. I'd upgraded to a sporty, all-weather style, but even it couldn't keep out the harsh Russian wind.

It didn't take long for Igor to get us suited up in heavier, windproof jackets. He handed over helmets with plexiglass face shields.

"You'll want them when you're going fast." He patted one of the white snowmobiles at his side. "These are the fastest ones in the area. Be careful."

I nodded and shoved the helmet onto my head, then turned to Cass. "Safety first."

"Yep." She pulled her helmet over her red hair and grinned at me.

I glanced at Pond Flower, who still hadn't left my side. "Do you want to ride or run?"

She gave the snowmobile a doubtful look—I swore she could understand me—then trotted a few feet away.

"Run, it is."

The sun was creeping toward the middle of the sky as we each climbed onto our own snowmobile. Days were short here, so we'd have to go fast to cover as much ground as possible. Zoya refused to travel in the dark, and I couldn't blame her.

"Bring them back safely!" Igor shouted.

Unlikely. But we could pay him for the vehicles if we didn't manage to return them.

"Ready?" Roarke asked.

"Like a cat's ready for tuna," I said.

"We can go." Zoya pointed ahead toward the open tundra. "Stay behind me at all times. We shouldn't encounter any difficulty today. We just need to make it to the safe house about five hours away. Then we sleep and start again when it is light."

She revved her engine. The thing roared, a beast of steel and oil. Snow sprayed as she peeled away. We followed, a single line of five snowmobiles and one hellhound who looked as if she were having the time of her life in the snow. Nix followed Zoya, with me behind, then Roarke, followed by Aidan and Cass. Pond Flower pulled up the rear, but my frequent glances back showed she had no trouble keeping up the pace.

The wind was bitter cold as we traveled, but it was bearable in the thick jacket and helmet that Igor had given me. Snow began to pelt against the plexiglass face shield.

Magic shivered over my skin as we raced across the snow, prickly and light. Did anyone else feel that? But it felt like it was coming from below me—from the snow itself. Was it my ice power?

Something was wrong. I could feel it. My magic was sending up the alarm that there was something beneath the snow. I didn't know how I knew, but I did.

I was about to shout out a warning when the world exploded in front of me. Snow burst into the air as steam and water shot up from below. The scent of sulfur burned my nose. The geyser went off right below Nix's snowmobile, throwing her and the vehicle high into the air. She flew up hundreds of feet, propelled by the water.

Shit!

My mind scrambled with how to fix this, but I had no magic that would work that high up. Could I use my telekinesis to manipulate Nix's body? She was limp against the machine—unconscious. She couldn't even conjure something to save herself.

Fear chilled my skin to ice.

"Nix!" I cried.

By now, she was falling, having lost her grip on the snowmobile. She was over two hundred feet in the air. The fall would kill her.

Behind me, Roarke's magic surged, the scent of sandalwood even stronger. He lunged into the air, his form dark against the stark white snow and pale sky. His powerful wings carried him toward Nix.

My heart lodged in my throat. Roarke grabbed Nix out of the air, shooting away from the geyser and the falling snowmobile.

I sagged with relief, but winced when the snowmobile finally hit the ground. It crunched, metal bending and contorting.

That could have been Nix.

Instead, she was safely in Roarke's arms as he flew her back to us. Up close, I could see her limp form and reddened skin. The steam had burned her.

Roarke landed with a thud in front of me. I hurried over.

"She's breathing," he said, concern creasing his brow. "Burns don't look like more than first or second degree."

Aidan strode up, Cass at his side. Pond Flower followed. Worry shined in all their eyes, even Pond Flower's.

"Can you heal her?" I asked, heart pounding. Nix looked so weak and small, her clothes wet from the steam and her skin a shiny pink.

"I think so." Aidan laid his hands on Nix, one on her shoulder and one on her thigh. The evergreen scent of his magic welled as he fed his healing power into her.

Tension thrummed in the air as we waited, desperate for him to heal her.

In the distance, I could see Zoya walking a circle around our small group, reaching down to touch the snow. Confusion etched her face.

I turned back to Nix, holding my breath. Her skin slowly began to turn a more normal shade, and her eyes fluttered open.

"Holy shit," she murmured. "That was wild."

"The geyser hit right under your snowmobile," Roarke said. "The metal protected you from the worst of the water. But the steam got you."

She winced. "Yeah. I can feel that."

"It'll be gone in a moment." Aidan finished doing his thing, feeding his healing energy into her. He finished it off by holding his hands about six inches from her clothes and conjuring a flame that dried her clothes.

When she was healed and dry, Roarke set her down. She swayed only briefly before righting herself.

Oh, thank fates. Relief weakened my muscles. Cass sagged against Aidan for support.

"Thanks, guys." She glanced over at her broken snowmobile. "Can I hitch a ride with one of you?"

"Me," I said, giddy that she was okay.

"Thanks."

Zoya approached, concern creasing her brow. "This isn't good. In the years since I've left, they've increased the perimeter of protective spells. We shouldn't have encountered any until tomorrow."

"You think this was part of the magical barrier and not just natural?" I asked.

"Geysers are normal in this part of Russia. But there shouldn't be any right here. We triggered something."

"So they could be anywhere?" Roarke studied the landscape around us.

"Exactly." Zoya frowned. "And we have no way to sense them."

"Maybe we do." I bent and picked up a handful of snow, studying it. "I have ice magic. Part of that gift is sensing heat or other changes through the ice. I felt a tickle of magic right before the geyser got Nix. I was about to shout a warning, then boom."

"So you could lead us," Zoya said. "And feel out for any trouble."

"I can try."

"I don't like it," Roarke said.

"There's no other choice." Zoya pointed in the direction we'd been traveling. "We have to go that way. Flying isn't an option, and the border of protections will form a circle around all of Oriamor. We must pass through danger no matter what."

"It's fine," I said. "I can do it."

I hoped. I knew Roarke didn't want me risking my life, but he was going to have to get used to the fact that it was my job. And I liked my job.

We climbed back on our snowmobiles. Nix got on behind me and wrapped her arms around my waist. I cranked the key in the ignition and took off, slowly at first so I could get a feel for the terrain. I stretched my magic out toward the snow, feeling for any change in the ground beneath me.

It took a moment, but I finally got ahold of it, seeing the ground beneath me like a strange heat map in my mind. There were areas of extra warmth that I avoided—geysers just waiting to blow if we went over them.

Once I had a feeling for where the geysers were, I revved the engine and took off, my heart singing. This might be dangerous, but it was like an icy version of riding Scooter and I loved it.

We cut across the snow, zigging and zagging around threats that only I could sense. In the distance, a geyser shot off, a magnificent spear of water that went straight into the sky. More geysers began to go off, as if they were angry that we were avoiding their traps. Steam filled the air and snow melted all around us, but we managed to stay ahead of the danger by seconds.

When we finally escaped the geyser field, my heart was pounding. We rode for over an hour before something began to feel weird again. Something in the snow felt off, but I couldn't place it. I pulled my snowmobile to a stop.

Zoya rode up next to me and shoved up the plexiglass face plate. "There's something ahead. I feel it."

"Me too. Any idea what?" I asked.

"Just looks like tundra to me," Nix said.

It was all I could see, too, with a scattering of silver birch trees and snowy volcanos in the distance. At least those were dormant. Lava was the last thing I wanted to deal with right now.

"Nix, can you conjure a rock?" Zoya asked.

"Uh, sure." The light floral scent of Nix's magic swelled on the air, then she handed a rock the size of a baseball to Zoya.

Zoya stood and chucked the rock as far as she could. It landed about thirty yards away. Then the ice shattered beneath the rock, and the snow dropped away. The sound was enormous, like the earth was cracking in two. It echoed across the land, making my ears hurt.

A great crevasse had opened up, dark blue and glowing.

"Shhhit," Nix breathed.

"Yeah. That'll kill a person," I muttered.

"It's a drop floor trap," Zoya said. "We can't see where the snow will disappear from. There's a pathway through, but danger on all sides."

"Can you sense where the snow will fall away?" Roarke asked.

I focused my magic, reaching out toward the ground in front of me. All I got was an unclear sense that something was wrong. "Not really. There's no temperature change, so I can't tell where the danger lies."

"That's okay," Zoya said. "I can get us through."

"How?" Cass asked. "I thought you said you gave up your power when you ran."

"The closer I get, the better it works. If they accept me back amongst them, I may regain all of my power. Then I could use it anywhere." Zoya stood again and held out her hand, palm facing the snowfield. A blue light shined, shooting from her hand to the snow like lasers. The snow began to glow in blue patterns, dark and light.

"Whoa. Is that like sonar?" I asked.

"Kinda?" Zoya said. "I just have a gift for understanding the space around me, particularly if it is made of snow or ice. I couldn't sense the geysers because they were heat. But this is all cold. The dark blue spots are hidden crevasses beneath the snow. They are ice caves. The white path is the solid snow. Drive your snowmobile only on the white, or you're going for a long fall."

"Cool," I said.

"I'll lead this time," Zoya said.

She cranked her engine and headed toward the snowfield. Her magic stayed on the snow, glowing blue and lighting the way. We followed her in a single-file line.

My heart thundered in my chest as we passed the crevasse that she had created with Nix's rock.

The ground fell away steeply. The crack in the ground glowed dark blue as the ice wall stretched down into the earth. It was the most beautiful color I'd ever seen, but there was nothing but a frozen death waiting inside that crevasse.

Ahead of us, the patterns on the snow began to shift.

"The ground is changing!" I cried.

"That's new!" Zoya shouted. "Go top speed!"

Zoya revved her engine, shooting forward at top speed. I cranked mine and followed. My friends did so as well. But we weren't fast enough for the ice. It was shifting, the patterns of the drop floor changing with magic. Ahead of Zoya, her path began to turn blue.

Suddenly the ground cracked beneath her, that familiar sound of the earth breaking. The nose of her snowmobile began to tilt down. She was going to fall!

I threw out my hand and shot ice toward her, reforming the ground beneath her vehicle. I poured all my magic into it, creating a massive ice bridge. Her snowmobile gained traction and shot up the bridge and over.

We followed. Nix's arms tightened around me. My heart was stuck in my throat as we passed over the bridge I'd created. I prayed to the fates that my bridge would hold and we'd make it across.

Finally, we did. I glanced behind to see Roarke, Cass, and Aidan follow. Pond Flower had no trouble as she raced across. She'd long ago adopted her protective black flame. Nothing could hurt her in that form.

Though the danger in the ice continued to shift, we made it off the ice field five minutes later. Once on solid ground—revealed to us by Zoya's magic—we stopped our snowmobiles.

"Holy fates, that was terrifying." Nix sagged behind me.

"No kidding," I said.

"That wasn't normal," Zoya said. "They've advanced their protections in the years I've been gone. I've never seen a drop floor trap that moves."

"It's effective," Roarke said. "Without Del, we'd be two hundred yards deep in the ice right now."

"Yeah. Let's keep moving." Zoya nodded her head toward the sun, which was heading toward the horizon. "It'll be dark too soon. We need to get to the safe house before nightfall."

I did *not* want to know what came out after nightfall, so I nodded. Everyone else agreed, and we revved our engines and followed Zoya. The volcanos in the distance grew ever larger as we neared them. To our left, smaller mountains cropped up. In front of them, there were dark shadows on the ground.

Zoya noticed them, too, and veered her snowmobile away. We were still several hundred yards from the shadows, but I thought they were deep cracks in the earth. Not ice cracks, but down into the dark volcanic rock.

Fear raced along my skin, making goosebumps pop up. There was something about those cracks in the earth...

Red began to appear at the edges of the cracks. My gaze raced between the ground in front of me—so I didn't crash my snowmobile—and the cracks that seemed to be bleeding.

"Zoya!" I shouted.

"I see them!" Her voice drifted back over the sounds of the engines. "Gun it!"

We cranked the throttles, and the snowmobiles leapt forward at top speed. But that didn't stop the cracks in the earth from bleeding faster and seeping toward us.

"Holy fates!" Nix cried. "They're giant crabs!"

I glanced back toward the red that swept across the snow, growing ever closer. But it wasn't blood. It was a tide of massive red crabs—each the size of a pickup truck. They scuttled across the snow toward us, an endless wave. Black fangs protruded from their weird mouths, and black eyes glared menacingly. Their claws were huge and serrated.

"Demon crabs," I muttered. These were straight from hell—no way anyone would be serving these up with butter and lemon.

"They're magic! A spell!" Zoya cried. "But their bite is real!"

Some were faster than others, breaking away from the pack and nearing us. No way we could fight them all. We'd have to outrun them, beating off the fastest crabs who would drag us back to their brethren—if they didn't devour us themselves.

Behind me, Nix's floral magic swelled. Out of the corner of my eye, I caught sight of her bow. She fired at the nearest crab, her aim straight and true.

But the arrow bounced off its eye.

"Shit!" She fired again, but this one bounced off the other eye.

If the softest part of the crab was impenetrable, then there was no way we'd be able to fight them.

"Fire!" Zoya cried from ahead of us. "Only fire will destroy them!"

Of course. They were magical creatures of the land of ice, despite their blazing red shells.

Nix conjured a flaming arrow and shot at the nearest crab. He was only forty yards away now—this needed to work.

The flaming arrow sailed through the sky and plunged into the crab's black eye. It reared back on its hind legs, then toppled over onto its shell. I winced, hating to see any animal killed. Though the crab wasn't truly real since it was made of magic. But it still looked awful. And it would have torn my flesh from my bones and devoured me, so....

I was okay with it.

Quick as a flash, Nix fired off more arrows. Though she was fast, there were too many crabs for her to hold off. Pond Flower threw herself into the fray, her protective black flame surrounding her. She lunged for a crab, who tried to snap her with its claw. She dodged nimbly, then went for his face. When her black flame touched the crab, it scuttled backward. She chased it away.

Aidan and Cass, both of whom possessed the gift of fire, shot jets of flame at the crabs, creating a barrier between us and them. Combined with Nix's arrows and

Pond Flower's black flame, we had just enough to hold off the barrage until we were far enough away that they stopped attacking.

We'd gotten out of range of the spell.

My breath came hard and fast as relief welled in me.

"That was close," Nix muttered.

Pond Flower loped along beside me, delight in her flame-red eyes. She was really enjoying this. More than me, to be honest. I liked a good adventure, but this was too deadly. Thank fates we'd brought Zoya.

"We're close to the safe house!" Zoya called back.

"Thank fates," Nix muttered.

"No kidding."

In the distance, the woods thickened. The silver birch trees gleamed white in the light of the setting sun. We only had about ten minutes of daylight left, I guessed. I didn't want to be trapped out on this tundra in the dark.

CHAPTER SIX

We slowed our snowmobiles as we traveled through the woods, finally coming upon a small cottage built of dark brown wood. Smoke billowed from the chimney. Zoya's friend must already be here.

We pulled to a stop near the front. As I climbed off, my legs shook like jelly.

"What an adrenaline rush," I muttered.

"I feel it too," Nix said. "I think my heart has been going a mile a minute for the last five hours."

Pond Flower perked up, her ears pricking high and her nose sniffing. Then she ran toward the side of the house. A crowd of big white huskies ran from behind the house, meeting her in a cluster. There were over a dozen of them, and all were fluffy as cotton balls.

"Huskies?" I asked Zoya.

She nodded. "Yeah. We can't take the snowmobiles from here. Too loud. Vera brought us sleds and dogs."

"Wow." I'd never ridden in a dogsled before. The huskies were huge—each the size of Pond Flower, who was already unnaturally large. Their blue eyes were fiercely intelligent as they greeted Pond Flower with the usual butt sniff.

Even magical dogs couldn't resist.

The door to the cabin opened, and a small, dark-haired woman came out. Her clothes were all black tactical wear, as if she were a Navy SEAL or something. Not exactly what I'd expect from an Ice Fae. Shouldn't she be wearing a glittery blue dress like Elsa?

Instead, she looked like a tiny package of death, able to take care of business in silence with no one the wiser.

She ran for Zoya, embracing her tightly.

"I thought I'd never see you again!" Vera cried. Her dark eyes shined with tears.

Zoya hugged her tight. "I always wanted to come back, but couldn't."

"I know." Vera stepped back.

The understanding on her face made me think that there was more to Zoya's story than I knew, but I wouldn't press her for it. None of my business.

"Come inside."

We followed Vera into the house. It was bigger than it had looked on the outside, with an open kitchen, living room, and several doors leading off into bedrooms. It was rustic and simple, but homey, with a fire burning in the fireplace and a pot of something savory bubbling on the stove.

Vera turned to us. "You're here to help with the demons."

"Yes," I said.

"Good." Vera nodded. "Let's have vodka, then discuss."

Apparently Russian Ice Fae were as into vodka as Russian humans. I had no problem with that.

My friends and I took off our coats and other warm layers, then hung them on hooks by the door.

I caught a whiff of my own scent. Sweat. "Ick. I smell."

"We all do," Nix muttered. "Lots of stress and heavy snowsuits do not make for a lovely potpourri."

"There's a hot spring out back that you can bathe in later," Zoya said.

"Thanks." I would definitely be making use of that.

"Help yourself to stew," Vera said as she pulled a couple of bottles of vodka from the small refrigerator and put them on the table.

I followed my friends to the big pot on the old stove, then filled my bowl with a savory combination of vegetables and broth. Surreptitiously, I poked around the bowl to see if there was any meat in it. It looked mostly like root vegetables, so I was probably good. I tore off a hunk of bread from the loaf on the counter, then joined my friends at the table.

Zoya sat next to me, reaching over to grab a bottle of vodka. She poured shots into the little glasses, then passed them around.

"We'd be sunk without you," I said to her. "Thank you for the help."

She nodded, her face grave. "I owed it to my people. They are in trouble, and you are the people who can help."

"I hope so." My stomach growled, so I ate a bite of the stew. It was hot and rich. Amazing. I chowed down.

Vera gave us time to eat and rest, but as soon as I'd finished my bread and soup, she raised her glass of vodka and looked at us all.

I took the cue and raised mine. Everyone else did as well.

"To closing the portal," Vera said.

We drank. The vodka burned on its way down—this was no boxed merlot—but it felt appropriate.

"So, tell us what's going on," Zoya said.

"The demons have taken control of our village," Vera said. "We were prepared for it. The prophecy said this would happen, so we had a plan in place. They believe that we are on their side because it's the only way for us to stay alive. And for me to leave with the dogs. But we aren't on their side, and we're ready to fight. We were planning our attack when you contacted us, Zoya."

"Good thing I did," Zoya said. "Unless we close the portal, you'd be fighting until you died. There will be an unending stream of demons."

"How many demons have flooded out already?" I asked.

"Thousands."

I dropped my glass. It thudded to the table, thankfully sturdy enough that it didn't shatter. "Thousands?"

Vera nodded, her face grave.

"Where are they?" Roarke asked, his voice sharp and serious.

"Gone." Vera shrugged. "There are a couple hundred in the village at any given time as they adjust to Earth. Eating our food, taking our beds. But they soon leave, scattering across the globe."

I slumped back in my chair, devastation a wasteland within my chest. Holy shit. Thousands. I thought hundreds, perhaps. Not thousands.

"How many demons are normally on Earth?" Cass asked. "Not that many, right?"

"There are a couple hundred demons dispersed on Earth at any given time," Roarke said. "They're primarily mercenaries taken from hell by sorcerers with the power to help them cross over. Once on Earth, they have jobs that they were brought here for. It keeps the mayhem at a manageable level."

"Now we have thousands," I said. "And all of them are running free, with the Shadows as their only boss."

"And the Shadows want you dead," Aidan said.

"Along with other things," I said. "Which we'll need to figure out."

"Later," Vera said. "The first job is to close the portal. Cut them off and keep their numbers as low as possible."

Thousands of demons was never going to be a low number. But I nodded. She was right. One problem at a time. Then we'd take this to the government. There was no choice. We were in over our head.

And *I'd* gotten us here.

I'd thought closing the portal would be my big battle. Nope.

Fighting thousands of demons was definitely the big one. And we still had to close the portal before we could even consider it.

"Are the Shadows in the village?" I asked.

She shook her head. "No. They came through already and are gone."

"Damn. Are you sure we can't leave now?" I asked. "To get there sooner?"

Vera's eyes hardened. "Absolutely not. We'll never make it in the dark. Not only are the traps hard to find, there are night monsters."

Great. After the magical giant crabs, I wasn't going to argue.

"We will leave right at first light," Vera said. "My people will help you however we can."

"Thank you," I said.

"Could you use your gift to turn back time right at the portal?" Nix asked. "You could go all the way back to when the portal was first formed and stop all the demons from ever coming out at all. Two birds with one stone."

It was so tempting to try it. I could almost taste it.

I met Roarke's gaze. Worry and skepticism darkened his eyes as he said, "I don't think it's a good idea."

I nodded. "He's right. It's been days that the portal has been open. Turning back time and changing history is forbidden. It's so dangerous."

"Having all those demons out there is dangerous," Nix said.

"You're right. But who knows what they've done while they've been out there? Bad things, yes. But sometimes bad inspires the greatest good. What if there's someone out there who is being inspired to become a hero in the future?"

"I don't know." Doubt shadowed Nix's voice.

"It's not that far-fetched. Think of us. Our time in the Monster's prison was horrible. But it brought us together and formed our future. And the world needed us to be together, so we could do the things we do."

Understanding lit Nix's gaze. "That's a good point."

An idea flared in my mind. "Cass, why don't you call Aethelred. Have him scry to see if there's any harm in us turning back time at the portal. I'm convinced it's a bad idea, but having a second opinion will make us feel better."

"Good idea." Cass pulled her cell phone from her pocket and punched in the numbers. She waited a few moments, and I heard the low rumble of Aethelred's voice grumbling about something.

Cass offered to pay him, then asked our question. There was a long silence. I had another shot of vodka as we waited, my nerves totally on edge. The liquor burned its way down my throat, warming my belly.

"Yeah, yeah. Okay." Cass nodded as she talked to Aethelred. "A few minutes? Okay, great. Thank you."

She hung up the phone and looked at the crowd. "Our resident seer says that Del is right. Aethelred wouldn't tell me what would happen if we turned back time, only that it was a terrible idea in the long run. Extremely dangerous."

"Damn." Nix sagged. "That would have been great."

Disappointment filled my chest too. Nix was right. It would have been the safest, easiest way to fix this.

"But he did say that we could turn back time a couple minutes. There shouldn't be as much risk there, since it's such a short amount of time. You're only turning back time at the portal, and those demons will only just have gotten onto Earth. They won't have had enough time to get out and change history."

"Every little bit helps, right?" I looked around the table. "We might as well do that."

"Agreed," Roarke said. "No large scale turning back time, but if Aethelred says that a few minutes is okay, we'll do that."

"Perfect," Vera said. "You'll close the portal. We'll save our village."

I smiled, trying to keep the worry off of my face.

After we'd cleaned up our dishes, I went with Nix and Cass for the first round of baths in the hot springs. The night air was freezing when we stepped outside, hurting my lungs as I drew it in.

But the sky was spectacular. Brilliant sweeps of green and yellow stretched across the sky, dancing and swirling. They cast a low glow on the silver birch trees in the forest. The rest of the night was black.

"The northern lights," Cass murmured.

"Amazing." I'd never seen them before. This had to be a good luck sign.

Pond Flower lay in the snow, gazing up at the lights. She looked so happy.

I grinned at her, then followed Cass and Nix along the path to the hot springs. The snow was tamped down, making it easier to walk.

The spring was only about five yards from the back of the house. The clear water gleamed green and yellow, reflecting the northern lights. Rocks surrounded it, a natural fissure in the ground. There was a wooden box near the side of the pool. I brushed the snow off, then put my towel on the top.

I looked at the snow, then my *deirfiúr*. "We're going to have to make this quick."

"No kidding," Cass said.

As fast as I could, I stripped out of my clothes and climbed into the water. My feet were icy from standing in the snow for even a second, so the water burned hot and fierce. But as I sank into the depths, my muscles relaxed and my skin adjusted.

"That's amazing," I sighed.

"No kidding." Nix sat on the rock next to me.

"It's like a natural hot tub," Cass said. "Except a bit more precarious."

She was right. We had to perch on rocks that were basically like benches, but not quite. However, the silver birch trees and northern lights more than made up for the lack of comfortable seating. I'd take this any day. It was even nicer than Roarke's fancy grotto bathroom.

I shifted around, finally finding a comfortable spot and leaning my head back against the rock to watch the northern lights.

"Why do you think we were chosen to be the three sides of the Triumvirate?" I asked.

Cass blew out a breath. "Whew. No idea."

"I think it's because we're worthy," Nix said.

"Cass is," I said. "She's already finished her part."

"Not really," Cass said. "I finished my part, but my job isn't done yet. We're each part of the whole. Without one of us, the whole thing fails. So my job isn't over until yours is. I couldn't have defeated the Monster without you. So now it's my turn to help."

She had a good point. Without her, I wouldn't have made it through many of these challenges. Same with Nix.

"I think that's why," Nix said. "We're powerful and fated to have some seriously strong magic, but it's also that we're a team. Like you said about our time with the Monster joining us together. We're an unbreakable bond. And when it comes to fighting big battles, we're three for the price of one. We each have our big job to do, but we have the others to help us."

I grinned, looking down from the brilliant night sky and meeting the gazes of my *deirfiúr*. "I like that."

"Me too," Cass said. "We're a team."

"Always have been," I said.

"Always will be," Nix added.

We cleared out of the hot spring not much later. The guys still hadn't had a chance to get cleaned up, and I was suddenly so sleepy I couldn't keep my eyes open. A combo of exertion, fear, stew, vodka, and a long soak in a hot tub had made me feel like a noodle.

We all bedded down on the couches and in spare bedrooms. They were rustic and small, but the beds were warm and the walls kept out the wind, so it was perfect for me. I took a smallish double bed and passed out.

Sometime later, Roarke joined me, but I was too tired to do much more than snuggle into him like a heat-seeking missile that moved super slowly.

Reality shifted from dark slumber to dreams. The blackness of my eyelids gave way to an image of my mother, sitting by the fire. She was rocking in a chair, reading a book. Just seeing her made me happy, as if I knew she'd give me a hug.

Closer inspection revealed that she was semitransparent. Ghostly. Nearby, a small portal glimmered. It looked like a portal to the Underworld—like the kind outside of Roarke's house in Magic's Bend.

So this wasn't the past. Which made sense, since my mother from the past would never hug me. Nor would she sit in a rocking chair by the fire. But perhaps it could be the future?

Now that my mother had realized how the dark magic of the Underworld had affected her, might she want an actual relationship with me? She'd shaken off the yoke of evil and was trying to convince my father that they'd made a mistake in helping the demons. If I was strong enough and smart enough to fix the problems facing me, perhaps I could use my portal skill to visit with my parents.

CHAPTER SEVEN

The next morning, after a quick but hearty breakfast, we geared up and went outside to greet our rides. The sky was just starting to turn gray as the sun approached the horizon. The air was bitter cold, nipping at my exposed cheeks.

Vera had been up early, feeding the massive huskies, and they were now bright-eyed and bushy-tailed, ready to start the day.

All sixteen of them milled around the yard, excited to run. Pond Flower milled with them, seeming delighted to be hanging out with other dogs. Because she'd kept me company for the last couple days, she hadn't been back to see her hellhound buddies.

Vera clapped her hands and shouted something in a foreign language. The huskies perked up, then ran to their sleds and got in formation. Four to each sled, which seemed like a small number, but they were truly massive dogs.

Vera hooked them up, then gestured us toward the sleds. "Two per sled. No need to steer, the dogs know what they are doing."

Wanting a cue for how to board the sled, I watched Vera and Zoya climb onto theirs. They both sat down, one in front of the other. There were no handles on the back like I'd seen on other dogsleds in photos, so Vera was serious when she said no one had to stand in the back and steer.

Following the Ice Faes' lead, I got on a sled with Roarke, sitting right in front of him. There was a heavy blanket, so I pulled it up on top of me, snuggling deep. Aidan and Cass boarded another sled, and Nix got on her own. Pond Flower jumped on behind her, barking happily. Apparently she was a diva, wanting to be pulled by her doggie brethren.

"*Har!*" Vera shouted, and the dogs took off. They were so fast that I slammed back against Roarke.

"Wow!" I grinned.

The dogs raced through the trees, nearly silent except for the thud of their paws and the swoosh of the sled through snow. They knew just where they were going and were fast as a bat out of hell.

The huskies pulled us through the forest and across the tundra, but the fun really started when we began to ascend the first snow-covered volcano. Though it was dormant—for now—I swore I could feel the heat beneath the snow.

The dogs barely slowed their pace as they pulled us up the steep side. We climbed higher and higher, then crested the top and began our descent. Going downhill, the huskies sprinted even faster. Wind bit into my cheeks and made my eyes water.

"I should have kept the snowmobile helmet!" I shouted back to Roarke.

"No kidding!" He wrapped his arms tight around me.

When we reached the valley between two volcanos, the dogs slowed. Their heads turned left and right, searching. Their noses twitched as they sniffed the air. The fur on their backs stood up. Pond Flower gave a gruff bark.

"Trouble," I muttered, searching the snowy valley.

To our left, dark shapes moved against the ground.

"*Har!*" Vera shouted, and the dogs picked up the pace.

I squinted toward the dark shapes, realizing that they were bears. Grizzly bears climbing out of their caves and thundering right toward us. There were twenty at least, and as they neared, I realized that they were massive. Even bigger than the crabs. And worse, they didn't feel like dark magic. They just felt like giant bears.

Who wanted to eat us.

But even though they planned to turn us into breakfast, I really didn't want to kill them.

"*Har!*" I cried at the dogs, figuring it meant faster. I'd rather outrun the bears than hurt them.

But they were fast. Soon, I could see their black eyes and yellowed fangs. Their huge paws pounded in the snow, kicking it up.

"Do we fight?" Aidan yelled.

"Not unless we have to! Wait for my signal." Vera cried. *"Har!"*

The dogs ran as fast as they could, but it wasn't fast enough. The grizzlies thundered in front of us, trying to cut us off. With a burst of magic that smelled like clean dog fur, the huskies put on a burst of speed and swerved around the bears, slipping past them.

The beast nearest me swiped out a paw, going for my middle. I dodged away, leaning out over the other side of the sled. The bear's claws missed me by an inch. I almost fell out, but Roarke dragged me back on.

I spun around to see if we'd made it past the bears completely. None of our sleds had been stopped and my friends were all safe, but the grizzlies had spun on a dime and raced after us.

They were fast—unnaturally so, just like the dogs. Unfortunately, our huskies were tired. The bears were gaining. Their fangs flashed, and their eyes gleamed.

"We're not going to make it!" My mind raced. I needed something not deadly.

Desperately, I called on my ice magic, letting the cold flow through me. I hurled my power at the bears, forming a wall of ice between us and them. Through the semiopaque surface, I saw them scramble in the snow, pulling to a halt before they slammed into the ice wall. They studied it for a moment, then roared their displeasure as they turned and raced around the side of it to continue the hunt.

But the delay had given our dogs enough of a head start. Though the bears tried to catch us, they couldn't make up the distance.

"Well done!" cried Vera.

I grinned, thankful to have gotten away without hurting them. I was glad that Vera didn't want to kill them either. She was a good egg.

The hours passed as the dogs carried us up and over mountain after mountain. Finally, we ascended the tallest mountain yet and stopped at the top, our sleds lined in a row. Deep in the valley below, ice glittered like massive crystals.

"That is the entrance to our village," Vera said.

"I don't see any houses," I said. "Just the ice."

"They're underneath. The ice protects us." Vera turned back to her dogs. "*Har!*"

The dogs burst into a run. We sailed down the mountain, ever closer to the glittering ice. As we pulled to a stop, I studied the ice formations in front of us. They were massive, geometric spears and pillars that jutted out of the earth in all directions. There were millions forming a maze-like forest that prickled with protective magic. It looked like an enormous thicket made of ice.

Vera climbed out of the sled and turned to face us. "We will part soon. I will take the dogs and return them. Zoya will stay with you. She cannot see the council before this is over."

Or they'd kill her for leaving. Wasn't that what she'd said? Did she hope that by helping to close the portal and thereby saving the village, that they would forgive her? It was a good plan. I just hoped we'd manage to help her see it through.

We climbed out of the sleds. I patted each dogs' head, thanking them for pulling us.

"You will need magic to protect you," Vera said. She approached me and raised a hand. It glowed with blue light like Zoya's had when she'd revealed the drop floor trap in the snow yesterday.

Vera held her hand in front of my face, then slowly lowered it down my body, hovering a few inches from my skin. Everywhere her hand passed, my skin chilled.

"Whoa," Cass whispered.

"What?" I asked.

"You look awesome," she said.

"Seconded." Nix grinned. "I want the same makeover."

Vera smiled. She was apparently done with me, because she turned and gave Nix the same treatment. I no longer felt cold, but I didn't feel normal either.

As Vera ran her hand down Nix's body, Nix began to turn sparkly and semitransparent. She looked like glittering ice. Even her dark hair turned white and translucent.

"That's freaking amazing," I murmured.

"I'm turning you into one of us," Vera said. "Temporarily, of course. Otherwise, the ice would recognize you as an outsider and keep you from entering. Until the council approves of you, you can't cross the barrier without being killed."

"Killed?" Roarke asked.

"Yes." Vera finished with Nix, then turned toward the ice spears that created the strange forest in front of us. She drew a dagger and nodded toward the daggers strapped to Cass's thighs. "Hold one of your daggers with your bare hand, then throw it between the ice towers."

Cass tugged off a glove and did as she requested, removing one of her sheathed obsidian daggers and throwing it expertly at the ice forest. As the blade passed between two of the ice spears, they snapped together like the jaws of a snake, trapping the dagger within.

"It would crush your flesh," Vera said. "You'd become human soup beneath the ice."

"Ew." I made a face.

"Makes my point though, doesn't it?" Vera asked.

"Sure does." I admired my clear, sparkling arm. "I like the look anyway."

Vera transformed all of us, even Zoya and Pond Flower, then turned to face us. "Zoya will lead you to an overlook where you can see the portal. As soon as you have closed it and no more demons are coming through, we will help you fight the demons who are still in the city. We must kill them all and free my people."

I nodded. "Thank you."

"No, thank you." Vera's gaze turned grave. "But you *must* succeed."

No kidding.

She turned and started toward the ice. As she neared the first row of spears, her opaque human body shifted into her Ice Fae form. She glittered as clear and bright as the rest of us, passing through the ice with no problem. The dogs shifted as well. It was one of the coolest things I'd ever seen as they trotted through the deadly pillars of ice.

My heart thundered as I followed Vera and Zoya between the first pillars of ice. But when they didn't snap closed and crush me, I relaxed slightly.

After that, I just admired the view as we passed between and under the jagged piece of ice. They twinkled clear and white as the sun sparkled through them.

Zoya gestured to us. "Come."

We veered off, following her away from Vera and the dogs. She led us toward a small overlook. The jagged crystalline spears formed a bit of a barricade for us. In our glittery, transparent forms, we blended very well. It was a good hideout even though we were very close to the village. We were right over the buildings' roofs, so close that I could call out and they would hear me.

The village was lovely, with buildings made of pale gray stone and streets paved in a similar material. The people within glittered icy clear like we did, their pale hair flowing on a light breeze. It was magical, in the truest sense of the word. I was used to the fantastic, but this was something special.

The portal at the right side of town ruined the whole thing, though. We were right above it and slightly in front. The thing was gaping and black, emitting an evil that made me shiver. A steady stream of demons flowed through, though I couldn't see any of the shadows anywhere. The demons were all shapes and sizes, every species. There was no similarity except that they all wanted to come to Earth and wreak havoc of the most horrible, violent variety.

"I guess I'll get to it," I whispered. "Everyone be ready to fight. The demons will know something is wrong as soon as the portal closes."

Everyone nodded, taking up battle stations. Down below, Ice Fae went about their business and the town looked normal. Well, as normal as a town could look when it was under demon occupation. I was ready to kick these jerks out of here.

I debated shifting into my Phantom form. It would protect me if battle broke out while I was working on the portal, but it was too dangerous. I would glow blue and bright, a beacon that gave away my location. It was better to stay camouflaged, even if it left me vulnerable.

I reached for my gift over time, letting it flow through me with a shiver. I directed it toward the portal, trying to keep it focused and narrow. It was imperative that I only turn back time right at the portal—not in the village itself. I didn't want to screw up anyone's life, after all.

I tried to envision the portal closing in the past, but it was difficult. Instead, I imagined the demons walking backward into the portal, as if they were being shown in rewind. It should happen in real life, too, I thought.

Unfortunately, turning back time like this felt nearly impossible. I couldn't get a grip on the magic. Though the theory was similar, it felt entirely different to imagining a long-dead temple and rebuilding it.

Sweat trickled down my temple as I pushed my magic harder, trying to force my vision into reality.

But it didn't work. I spent at least ten excruciating minutes trying to turn back time a couple minutes, but it was just too weird. Too wrong. Maybe the magic of the portal was preventing it? Or maybe I just wasn't strong enough to manage it.

"Hurry," Roarke whispered beside me. "Demons are starting to look suspicious. They may feel your magic influencing the portal."

I opened my eyes. Damn it, he was right. The demons looked around, studying the portal and then the land around them. Some even put their hands to their weapons.

"I can't turn back time here," I whispered.

"Just close it, then," Roarke murmured. "We can fight them."

I nodded sharply and shifted gears, calling upon my portal magic. I envisioned my mother briefly, picturing her as she told me to imagine my power as a light I could manipulate. I followed her advice, envisioning my portal magic as a golden light inside of me.

Slowly, it solidified, warming my chest from the inside and giving me the confidence to send my magic toward the portal, envisioning it closed and cutting off all the demons.

A shout nearly broke my concentration. Demons from below were turning toward us, looking up at the small cliff and pointing.

Had they seen us? I ignored them, focusing on my magic.

"Go time," Cass said. "We'll have your back."

Roarke squeezed my shoulder, then stepped away. From the corner of my eye, I could see the black tornado form around him as he shifted into his demon form. In a flash of golden light, Aidan shifted into his griffon form.

I kept my attention squarely on the portal as battle exploded around me. My friends leapt off the cliff, Roarke and Aidan carrying Cass and Zoya straight into the fray as demons surged toward me. Nix stood at the cliff edge, firing her arrows down at the demons below.

Roarke and Aidan dropped the others safely on the ground. Cass powered up her fire, throwing balls of flame at any demon who approached me on the cliff, while Zoya shot blue light from her palm that froze the demons solid. The Ice Fae were fighting as well, every one of them—old and young—armed with blades of ice. Some had Zoya's power, which was the fiercest of all.

My friends defended me from below, keeping the demons from climbing the thirty-foot cliff and stopping me from my work.

As Roarke swept through the air, tearing demons off the cliff wall, I pushed my magic toward the portal, envisioning it closing forever.

My skin prickled with adrenaline and fear as I drew on every bit of magic I had. Closing portals wasn't quick work, and this was the strongest portal in the world. But I didn't have time to doubt. We were outnumbered. I could see without even looking closely that the demons outnumbered the fae.

I forced my magic toward the portal, giving it everything I had. My breath came short, and my muscles quaked. A demon nearly breached the edge of the cliff as the portal began to shrink. He crawled up over and reached for me, but Roarke swooped up on powerful wings and dragged him away.

"Hurry!" someone cried.

I shook as I worked, but the portal was closing. Slowly, slowly, it shrank. The black was eaten away by the glittering white of the village returning to normal. The demons in hell must have known something was up, because they raced out of the portal as fast as they could.

The portal was nearly gone when something flew at me. I tried to dodge, but was slowed by my unwillingness to let go of the portal.

Pain flared in my upper arm. Some kind of weapon had hit me—a knife or an arrow, I hadn't been able to see. I debated adopting my Phantom form, but discarded the idea. I couldn't waste the magic or the mental energy. I needed all my focus to close the portal.

So I ignored the pain, giving everything I had to the job at hand.

Another projectile sliced through my side. Agony flared, like hot metal pressed against my bare flesh.

Shit, this was bad. I was a target now.

With a last burst of strength, I fed my magic to the portal. It took everything I had, making my heart race and dimming my vision to gray. Finally, the portal closed, zipping out of existence. The demons roared their rage as I stumbled, my muscles weakened and my head swimming. Pond Flower raced in front of me. I grabbed onto her for support, blinking to regain my vision.

I'd given everything I had to the portal and was so close to passing out. But Pond Flower's magic flowed into me, strengthening me. She was like my familiar, or something. I didn't understand it, but I was grateful.

"Del!" Roarke shouted from above. "Are you all right?"

"Yes!" Strength was flowing into me. I could see again, and my muscles were strong. Blood still dripped from the wounds in my arm and side, but I was fine.

I dragged in a ragged breath and adopted my Phantom form, taking stock of my surroundings. Nix continued to fire arrows down at the ground, never leaving her position at the cliff edge.

The battle raged below, demons fighting the Ice Fae and my friends. Bodies lay in the street. More demons than Ice Fae, but they were down too. My friends were wounded, blood dripping from cuts all over their bodies, but they were still fighting.

Cass was a whirlwind of fire, cutting through clouds of demons and taking them out like they were toys. Roarke swept through the air, grabbing up demons from the base of the cliff and breaking their necks. He nimbly avoided arrows and daggers that were thrown at him. Aidan flew as well, his powerful griffon form swooping low and grabbing up demons with his huge claws. He tore them to bits, raining blood onto the pale stone streets.

I leaned over the edge of the small cliff, shock piercing my chest. The thirty-foot cliff wall was covered in demons climbing up to stop me from closing the portal. Nix took out one every five seconds, but there were so damned *many*. Dozens more gathered at the base, scrambling to reach me. My friends were holding them off, but the demons would overpower them eventually. They'd overrun the cliff, taking me with them.

Then, they'd turn and demolish the village.

No way in hell I'd let that happen.

I backed up so the demons couldn't grab my ankles when they reached the top of the cliff and glanced around, frantic for a plan. I couldn't power up enough icicles to kill all the climbing demons quickly. Most of my power wasn't very handy as mass murder.

Except....

"Nix! Get back from the edge. Now!" I cried.

She hesitated, then lowered her bow and raced to my side. I eyed the towering spears of ice that had formed the barricade I'd hidden behind, then called on my new telekinesis. I envisioned the bases of the ice spears cracking and breaking, then the thousands of tons of ice plummeting over the small cliff and crushing the demons.

My muscles trembled as I forced my magic to follow my will. The sound of ice cracking was like music to my ears. It echoed with the noise of the battle below. When the ice began to tip, joy flared in my chest.

Demons were climbing over the edges of the cliff now, so close to me that I could smell their rank, evil magic.

"Watch out, guys!" I shouted to my friends. "Threat from above!"

The demons' wide eyes met mine and I grinned, giving my magic a last shove. At least forty massive ice spears toppled from the top of the cliff like a wall of death. I leaned over to look as the ice hurtled down the side of the cliff, taking out the demons in one fell swoop. The ice knocked them off the cliff and crushed them under its weight.

"Nice," Nix said. "You took out at least fifty."

"Let's take care of the rest."

Nix saluted and drew her bow. "Aye aye."

I found an ice spear that was propped against the cliff like one long slide. I climbed up and slid down into the fray, hitting the ground and rolling to my feet.

I called my sword from the ether and powered up an icicle in one hand. I threw the spear of ice at the nearest demon. It plowed through his middle, and he collapsed to the ground.

The battle raged around me, but it'd turned in favor of our side. I fired icicle after icicle as those around me fought tooth and nail. Pond Flower was vicious, along with the Husky friends. But it was the Ice Fae who really shocked me. Those who could freeze bodies solid didn't hesitate to use their power. There were demon popsicles all over the street.

When the last demon had died and the street fell silent, my head swam. Once again, pain flared in my side and arm. I finally looked down at the wounds, shock opening up a hole in my chest.

Blood soaked my entire arm and all of my side, reaching far down my leg. Fading adrenaline made me shake.

Holy fates, it looked like my wounds were worse than I thought. I spun, trying to find my friends. The pile of demon bodies underneath the massive pillars of ice caught my eye. The slanted pillar that I'd ridden to the ground was slicked with blood. My blood.

Oops.

I swayed, falling to my knees. Blood loss was finally getting to me.

"Del!" Roarke's voice echoed in my woozy head. Through blurry eyes, I saw him swoop down and land in front of me. He didn't look much better than I felt. He was covered in cuts and blood too. His gait was unsteady as he rushed toward me. He knelt at my side, but it was really more of a controlled collapse.

"We did it, right?" I slurred.

"Yeah." He wrapped an arm around me. My head spun from blood loss and pain.

I was going to say something, but we both crumpled to the ground.

CHAPTER EIGHT

I drifted in and out of consciousness. At the best of times, I saw a pale white light through slitted eyelids. At the worst, it was blackness. The pain in my wounds flared, then disappeared.

After what felt like a millennium, a voice woke me, pulling me from the darkness.

I blinked my eyes, finally strong enough to open them. It was blurry and white at first, then I focused on a figure. She was pale and clear, with the sparkling white hair and skin of the Ice Fae.

"I'm Gera, the healer." Her voice sounded like wind chimes. "You've had a bit of trouble with blood loss, but you'll be fine."

I struggled to sit up, feeling like I was pushing my way through jello. "Where are my friends?"

I searched the room, grateful to see Roarke seated in the chair next to me. Pond Flower was sprawled out on the floor next to him, snoring. A smile tugged at the corner of Roarke's mouth, and he reached for my hand.

The room itself was full of narrow beds draped in white fabric and tables full of potions and tools. A hospital?

"Your friends are fine," the healer said. "Many were wounded, but they are better now. Almost all of them are in the waiting room adjoining this one, having lunch."

A head popped in through the door. Cass. Then Nix. "You're up!" Nix cried. She had a sandwich in her hand.

"Thank magic," Cass said. "How do you feel?"

"A lot better." I looked at the healer. "Thank you."

"No, thank you. You saved us."

I doubted that, but didn't say it.

"Why don't you join your friends for a meal, then the council would like to see you," Gera said.

"Okay." I could definitely use some food before we faced out next big problem. And a big problem it would surely be—thousands of demons running lose was going to be hell to deal with.

After a quick lunch of sandwiches and soup—which were of an unfamiliar variety—Cass, Nix, and I made our way toward the main council hall with Pond Flower at our side. Both Roarke and Aidan had departed earlier with the intent of calling the Order of the Magica and the Alpha Council to see if they knew anything. We'd agreed to not reveal what we knew—yet—but it was time to gather more intel.

The streets of the village were quieter than they had been. Night had fallen, and it was cold and dark. The

Aurora Borealis did not grace us with its fantastic light show tonight. The bodies had been cleared from the streets, though there were still patches of blood staining the pale gray stone. Everyone was inside their homes, away from the cold and the site of so much death.

As we approached the large council chamber at the edge of town, I caught sight of Roarke and Aidan, each leaning against the wall of the building while talking into a cell phone. They waved at us, then returned their attention to the calls.

The building was built of the same gray stone as the others, but this one was two stories tall with a magnificent slanted roof. The doors were huge slabs of dark wood that opened at the slightest touch. Inside, it was one large room, warm and filled with golden light from sconces that lined the walls.

A long rectangular table sat in the middle of the room. It had space for at least thirty people, though it was only two thirds full. Everyone seated was an Ice Fae, their sparkling, transparent forms looking as icy as the snow on the mountains. Their magic smelled like an icy winter day, and a chill breeze rushed over me. I'd felt this magic before, during the battle, but had chalked it up to the weather. But inside this cozy room, it was obviously the magical signature of the Ice Fae.

Zoya and Vera sat near the head of the table, next to an older woman with the most commanding presence I'd ever seen. She even gave Madam Melephonus a run for her money. Her features were strong and ageless, though beautiful. She could have been thirty or fifty—it was impossible to say.

The woman rose, revealing that she was well over six feet tall and dressed in sweeping white robes. Her white hair was piled high on her head, and her eyes glittered a striking blue. I winced slightly. That gaze could see right into my soul, it seemed.

"Welcome." Her voice resonated with power, echoing off the high ceiling. "I am Galina, the council leader. Please, join us."

She gestured to seats along the side of the table, and we took them. Pond Flower lay on the floor behind us, apparently still loath to leave my side. There were two empty chairs beside us, but Roarke and Aidan walked in a moment later. Galina greeted them in the same way, and they sat next to us.

Twenty pairs of icy blue eyes turned in our direction. We weren't in trouble—I didn't think—but suddenly I felt like I was in the principal's office. I wasn't used to such scrutiny from a government body, even a small one such as this.

"We'd like to thank you for helping us save our village," Galina said. "Without you to close the portal, we would never have had a chance."

I almost mentioned that I'd been the one to open it, but that would have been plain stupid. Of course I felt guilty about it. But not enough that I'd fess up to Galina.

Instead, I said, "I wish we could have done more. I'm sorry for your casualties."

Sadness crossed Galina's face, her mouth turning down at the corners and her blue eyes darkening. "We lost good Ice Fae. But this event has been prophesied for generations. We knew to expect it. And in fairness, it was far less devastating that we expected it to be."

I remembered what Zoya had said. She'd been so afraid of this battle that she'd run from here. But now she was seated next to the boss lady, a look of contentment on her face. She was glad to be back. I smiled, happy for her.

"We must discuss the demons who have escaped," Galina said. "We do not want them roaming the earth freely."

I sat up straighter. "Yes. That is of primary importance to us. How many have escaped?"

"At least two thousand. Possibly closer to three," she said.

Damn. I'd hoped she'd say less than Vera had estimated, but of course the number was just as dire.

"All of the demons departed overland because our protective charms make it impossible to use transportation charms and teleportation," Galina said. "None of them spent long in our village. They forced us to escort them past the barriers, then they went their own way."

"What about their leaders?" I asked.

"Those shadowy figures have long since departed." Galina shuddered lightly. "We do not know where they went."

Double damn. I turned to Roarke and Aidan. "Did you guys learn anything from the Order of the Magica or the Alpha Council?"

Roarke gestured to Aidan. Aidan, as the Origin and strongest shifter, had contacts with the Alpha Council that no one else did.

"The Alpha Council does not know much." Aidan frowned. "They've seen more demon sightings, but had no extra trouble. However, they don't monitor demon activity with the same intensity that the Order of the Magica does."

The Order employed a band of bounty hunters and mercenaries to keep track of demon activity and send them back to hell when necessary—which was almost always.

"What about the Order, Roarke?" I asked.

"They knew a bit more, but not much. I wasn't able to press without revealing what I knew, which we haven't agreed to do yet. They did say that there has been an increase in demon sightings, but not an increase in activity. For all intents and purposes, the demons are behaving themselves."

"Well, that's not natural," Cass said.

"Certainly not," Galina said. "Though there are demons who are not evil, the ones that we've watched come through the portal are the worst of the worst. The kind who eat children and live off the fear of others. Murderers, slavers, and rapists. They stunk of dark magic. If they are behaving themselves now, it's not because they want to live a peaceful life on Earth. They have a plan."

"I'm inclined to agree with you," Roarke said.

"Same." I nodded. "After seeing the Shadows and the types of demons they employed, this isn't a peaceful move from the Underworld to Earth."

"Then they're planning something," Nix said. "The Shadows, most likely. And they're keeping their demon minions quiet for the time being."

"I would think so," I said.

"Agreed." Roarke nodded. "Their behavior is unusual. The Shadows won't be able to keep them quiet for long. Whatever they are planning—it's going to happen soon."

"Did the Order of the Magica say anything else?" Galina asked. Though she was a government official in her own right, her village was so remote that they didn't have any reason to engage with the worldwide government of supernaturals. Some species governed themselves, and a remote, closed-off one like the Ice Fae were one of those species.

"Not much," Roarke said. "Though they did say they were putting their top people onto figuring out what is wrong. If I visit them and share what we know, they're likely to help us. We both want the same goal."

We were going to have to show them ours if we wanted to see theirs. Of course. As much as it made me nervous to engage with the Order of the Magica—these were the people who hunted FireSouls, after all—we had no choice.

"Then you will meet with them tomorrow," I said. "Find out what you can. Then we come up with a plan for how to defeat the demons."

"We will help," Galina offered. The others around the table murmured their agreement. Zoya and Vera nodded.

"You've already suffered such great losses." Guilt pierced me at the idea of more Ice Fae dying.

"We will suffer more if we don't defeat the demons. There are thousands of them—you're going to need our help."

She was right. I nodded gratefully. "Thank you."

"Just tell us what you need, and we will deliver." She stood. "If everyone is satisfied, we will adjourn the meeting."

The crowded nodded in unison, murmuring their assent.

Galina looked at us. "You are welcome to stay here for the night if you like."

Cass and I shared a glance of mutual understanding—we wanted to sleep in our own beds, if possible. And since we were no longer with Zoya, who refused to travel via magical means, we could hopefully get out of here quicker.

I glanced at Roarke, asking with my eyes if he had a way to build and Underpath here. I *really* wanted to sleep in my own bed.

He nodded at me, then turned to Galina. "Thank you, though we would like to leave tonight. You said that it is impossible to use transportation charms or teleportation. But if you have a cemetery or a haunted place, I can create an Underpath. Do you think your protective charms will prevent us from using that?"

"What is an Underpath?" she asked.

Roarke briefly explained his ability to travel via the unique magical portals.

Her brows rose, interest glinting in her eyes. "That should be fine. The charms only prevent the use of the charms and teleportation because we don't want people popping in unexpectedly. But your skill is unheard of to us. We wouldn't have known to protect from that."

Worry creased her forehead.

"There's no need to protect from it," Roarke said. "I am the only one capable of creating an Underpath entrance, and I mean you no harm."

"Of course." Galina smiled, then led us toward the exit. Pond Flower followed along at her side.

Zoya hurried over, joining us. The group hesitated by the door, waiting so Zoya could say whatever she so obviously wanted to say.

"Thank you for asking me to bring you back here," Zoya said. Her southern accent had faded in favor of the lightly Russian one that the other Ice Fae shared. "I was afraid—it was the reason I ran in the first place—but that was selfish and cowardly. You helped me see that I needed to stand with my people."

"Thanks." I smiled at her. "Though I don't think I deserve the praise. I just needed your help."

"Well, however it happened, I'm glad that we met and that I came home." She shivered. "Though I'm not sure I want to live here permanently. The south is for me. But I'm glad to be reunited with my people."

Family was everything.

Zoya hugged me quickly, then returned to the table.

Without a word, Galina led us out of the building, and down the quiet street. Stars had begun to sparkle in the night sky, driving away some of the dark sadness that now cloaked the village. It was as if the stars promised that there was more than just us and death—we were part of something greater.

And we were.

Roarke hung at the back of the pack, tapping something into his cell phone. It took us ten minutes to reach the cemetery, which was on the other side of town in a beautiful spot. Sparkling headstones made of ice stood proud between silver birches. It was a nice place, quiet and pretty.

"Will this do?" Galina asked.

"Yes." Roarke put his phone in his pocket and turned to her. "Thank you."

Galina inclined her head. "Call upon us when you need us."

Without another word, she left, drifting through the cemetery woods, her cloak glittering white under the light of the moon.

It didn't take long for Roarke to create the Underpath. I insisted on being last to leave the village. One at a time, he took us through to Mad Mordecai's in Magic's Bend. Pond Flower waited with me, eventually teleporting herself to Magic's Bend when Roarke took me through the Underpath. When I stepped out of the smelly alley, my head still spinning from the journey, I caught sight of two big SUVs parked at the curb.

I looked at Roarke. "Is this who you were texting on the phone back there? Demon escorts?"

"Yeah. I didn't think we were keen on walking home."

"I know I'm not." I joined Nix in the second SUV. Pond Flower scrambled into the back.

The demon driver looked like a college kid, with a baseball cap and scruffy hair. His teeth were a bit pointier than they should have been, but otherwise, he blended well in regular society. I had to assume his hat covered his horns. His magic smelled like light beer and laundry detergent. Or maybe that was just him. Either way, he clearly wasn't evil like the demons we were hunting.

"Heya," he said, his surfer accent thick and out of place in Oregon. "We'll be there in a jiff."

Roarke climbed in next to me, and the kid pulled away from the curb and set the music to blaring. I wouldn't have heard my cell phone, but fortunately I'd set it on vibrate. The thing had 2 percent battery left, so I opened the messaging app to check the text I'd been sent.

Have answers about the stone. Meet me tomorrow morning, eight a.m. - Dr. Garriso.

I held it up for Roarke to read, my heart racing. "This is good news."

"Hopefully," he said.

I grimaced. "But if it were terrible, Dr. Garriso would have wanted me there sooner."

"Good point." He squeezed my hand. "You can go check on that while I visit with the Order. Then we'll reconvene."

"Perfect."

Our demon escort dropped us off at the curb in front of Ancient Magic. He pressed a button to automatically open the trunk, and Pond Flower leapt onto the ground. As I climbed out of the SUV, I took one last look at the kid before he pulled away. He really was nothing like the demons that we hunted.

I suddenly felt bad for my prejudice against demons when I'd first met Roarke. I'd thought that they were all bad. Heck, most people thought they were all bad. But that was because we didn't realize that there were so many decent demons living in hell, and even a few here on Earth. The problem was, the good ones kept such a low profile we didn't realize they existed.

That'd teach me to judge a group so quickly and harshly.

I reached for Roarke's hand and squeezed. I'd learned a lot from him.

"You okay?" he asked.

"Great." My smile twisted. "I mean, relatively speaking. I'll be better once this is all fixed."

Cass, Nix, and Aidan joined us on the sidewalk.

"Agreed," Cass said. "I'd like to get this sorted and then take a break. For years."

"Seconded," Nix said, then her smile faded. "Except that I still have my fated task to accomplish. And given that neither of yours have been exactly easy…"

"Let's not think about that," I said. "The Triumvirate business can wait. Let's do this one step at a time."

"And the next step is sleep." Cass grinned.

"Exactly." I gazed at the green door that led to our apartments, wanting nothing more than to crawl into bed. "Tomorrow I meet with the Collector to learn more about that magical rock. Roarke will meet with the Order to see if he can get more info. Then we can all meet in the afternoon and discuss our plan."

"We'll need to put it into action soon," Roarke said.

There was a chorus of "oh, yeahs," and "definitelies." No one wanted the demons hanging out any longer on Earth than they had to—and certainly not long enough to implement their plan, whatever that was.

We all headed up to our apartments for bed. Pond Flower followed me, padding up the stairs. Though I'd been spending a lot of nights over at Roarke's place, I wanted to sleep in my own bed tonight. Anyway—it was just up a flight of stairs. There was no way I was turning that down in favor of another car ride.

Though I toyed with a brief fantasy of jumping on Roarke as soon as we made it into my apartment, by the time I walked through the door, the exhaustion really hit me. As if being in a place that was safe allowed my system to shut down and relax.

Pond Flower hopped onto the couch and settled down for the night. That looked like a damned good idea.

"I'm so beat," I muttered.

"Likewise." Roarke followed me into the bedroom.

We managed to yank off most of our outerwear before tumbling into bed. I had just enough energy to press a kiss to his lips before falling asleep halfway on top of him.

CHAPTER NINE

The next morning at seven thirty, I hurried down the stairs alone. Roarke had left earlier to go meet with the Order of the Magica, but I didn't need to see Dr. Garriso until eight. I'd had to bribe Pond Flower to stay with Nix since she wouldn't fit on my motorcycle, and she definitely wouldn't fit in Madam Melephonus's treasure-filled house.

The morning was brisk and bright, the usual winter clouds having disappeared sometime in the night. I tugged on my helmet and hurried across the street toward Scooter. When I reached the motorcycle, I ran an affectionate hand over the handlebars. I'd been neglecting my bike lately, but once things were back to normal, I'd ride it more.

I couldn't freaking wait for life to be back to normal.

I swung a leg over the seat and cranked the ignition, then pulled away from the curb. Cold wind tore at my hair as I made my way to Dr. Garriso's office.

He met me in the parking lot.

"Good morning, Del!"

"Morning, Dr. Garriso." I climbed off Scooter and set my helmet on the seat. A spell would keep it from being stolen. All motorcycles sold in Magic's Bend came with that nifty feature. "Did Madam Melephonus give you any clues about what she found?"

His eyes twinkled. "Not a chance. She likes the limelight. She'll wait to reveal that herself."

"All right then." I joined Dr. Garriso in his stately sedan, and he drove us to the edge of the woods where Madam Melephonus lived. It was much easier to get past the enchantment this time, because now that she'd met me, she trusted me enough to give me the same "hall pass" that she'd given Dr. Garriso.

Once again, the pretty blue house had cats all over the porch. They lounged in the sun and shade, on cushions and on bare floor. It didn't look like such a bad life, being a house cat.

Mouse, the slender cat with midnight fur, waited for us on the stairs. Her keen yellow eyes examined us as we crossed the lawn, and she wasted no time in hurrying to Dr. Garriso and insisting that he pick her up. He did, then climbed the stairs and knocked on the blue door. Lurch let us in, and he looked as equally unimpressed with me as he had the last time. His brow was heavy over his dark eyes, which never so much as glanced at me.

I slipped by him and walked carefully down the hall, making sure not to brush against anything on the many shelves and send something priceless crashing to the ground. I really needed Madam Melephonus to like me long enough to tell me about the rock.

We took a seat on the delicate settee. Once again, Mouse leapt onto the wingback chair and began to clean her toes. Occasionally, she glanced up with wise yellow eyes that said *don't try any funny business.*

I should get a guard cat for my trove.

Madam Melephonus joined us shortly after. Once again, she wore a sequined-covered leisure suit and her colorful glasses. But this time, I didn't even think about considering her flighty. She carried a large wooden box in her hands.

"At least you're punctual," she said to me. For Dr. Garriso, she spared a sweet smile.

"You've learned something?" I asked.

She nodded as she set the box on the table under the window, then opened it. "Come and see."

I joined her, leaning over the box and gasping. "It's broken!"

The jagged black rock had split open to reveal a core of smooth, shining black glass. Obsidian?

"No." She shook her head as if I were an idiot. "It's open."

"Open?"

"Yes. The outer rock was just to protect the core."

"Is the inner rock obsidian?"

"It is. But this isn't how obsidian is found in nature. The rock has been imbued with magical properties. It is an amplifier—the most powerful ever known."

Of course. That's how it had made my power work. It'd taken what little unpracticed portal magic I had possessed, and amplified it into something that could be used to create the portal to Oriamor.

"Is it necessary to have a huge machine to make the amplifier work? I took it off of an ancient device."

Her brow arched as she gazed at me skeptically, and I realized what I'd said. It wasn't kosher to tear apart ancient artifacts.

"It's not how you think," I said. "The stone was being used to fuel a machine to open a terrible portal. We couldn't leave this in the hands of the people who had it."

Her dark eyes bored into mine as she considered my words. Then she nodded. "Fine. I won't give you a hard time. If Dr. Garriso thinks you're on the level, then so do I." She turned back to the rock, studying it. "And no, it doesn't need some kind of machine to make it work. A powerful enough supernatural can bend it to their will, amplifying any magic they want."

Then maybe the machine had been used to control me. Whatever it had been, I was glad we'd destroyed it.

"Thank you for figuring it out," I said.

"You must protect it." She ran a gentle finger over the gleaming back surface of the obsidian. "I'd offer to pay you for it, but I get the impression you won't accept."

I shook my head. "No. I think I'll need it. But I'll keep your offer in mind.

We might be able to use it to help defeat the Shadows. An amplifier could come in handy, especially one as powerful as this one was purported to be.

An hour later, I walked into P & P. Nix, Cass, and Aidan were waiting for me at our usual spot in the corner. Emile was there, too, with Ralph and Rufus on his shoulders. Cade sat next to him, having returned from his trip.

"Hey!" Connor called from behind the counter. "Take a seat, and I'll bring over your usual."

I hurried to my friends as Claire came out of the kitchen carrying a tray of pasties. She joined us, taking a seat next to me and setting the tray down for everyone. She pointed to one at the edge. "That's veggie."

"Thanks." I grinned at her, then grabbed it and bit in, burning the top of my mouth. "Ow ow ow."

"How'd it go with Madam Melephonus?" Cass asked as she juggled a hot pasty in her hands. She'd been too hungry to wait, too, it seemed.

"Good. I think we have a weapon we can use." Tentatively, I bit into the pasty. This time, I just got the savory taste of potatoes and carrots without the misery of a mouthful of steam.

Roarke walked in a moment later, his face unreadable. That couldn't be good.

He joined us, sitting on my other side and greeting everyone. Connor came out with a tray full of drinks and took the last chair.

The gang was together, so we could start.

"Well, tell us more about the rock," Nix said.

I told them about its amplifying powers and how it'd been trapped inside the protective shell of lava.

"And she said it's the most powerful in the world?" Roarke asked.

"She did." I sipped my espresso, grateful for the taste but not needing the caffeine. I probably wouldn't be able to sleep until this whole thing was over.

"Then we can definitely use that," Roarke said.

"What did you learn?" Aidan asked.

Roarke sighed and faced the group. "It's not good. They were only willing to share once I told them everything we knew—leaving out certain pertinent details, of course."

I assumed he meant our FireSoul natures and that he'd tried to shift the blame from me for opening the portal.

"Up until that point, they'd been aware that something was off," Roarke said. "But with my information, they were able to piece things together fully. Their intel suggests that the Shadows and their demon army are working to overthrow the Order of the Magica and the Alpha Council."

"They want to be in charge?" I asked.

"Unlikely," Roarke said. "They just don't want anyone in their way to stop them from doing whatever the hell they want. Those two governments are the only two bodies of supernaturals with the power and organizational skills to pose a threat."

"Except for us," Cass said.

I smiled at her. "Hopefully the Shadows don't realize that yet." I turned to Roarke. "Do you have any idea how they are planning to overthrow the government?"

"Not a clue. No one knows. They aren't even sure they're right about this, but it's their best guess for why the demons are lying low and congregating."

"Where?"

"All over. There are more than a dozen groups in different cities—all the evilest species of demons, but most of them reigning in their baser natures. For now. They don't want to draw attention."

"So we find them and kill them," Aidan said.

"We could, except they are constantly moving around," Roarke said. "And that's not the worst of it. After my meeting with the council, I visited my headquarters in the Underworld. Something is wrong, and it didn't take long to determine what."

Oh, shit. I'd never seen such a dire look on his face before.

"What is it?" My skin chilled as I waited for his response.

"With so many of the evilest demons out of the Underworld, the magical power balance is off, causing instability in the walls that separate the different realms. The Underworld is made of heavens and hells and neutral places. All of the religions are represented there, and they all make up part of the whole. The good magic from the heavens is balanced by the dark magic of the hells. Without the dark magic provided by the evilest demons…"

He searched for the right words, but I was too impatient. Worry was a beast clawing inside me.

"What's going to happen?" I demanded.

"Without enough evil to keep the Underworld as *the Underworld,* it may flip and become entirely a heaven. The barriers between the good places and the bad places will break down without the proper balance of magic to fuel them. Suddenly, there'll be bad demons in the heavens and neutral places. And since there is nowhere for the evil demons to go when they die—or even the evil humans—they'll just regenerate on Earth."

"And we'd never get rid of them," I said, my heart sinking.

"And we'd screw up the Underworld," Nix said.

"Oh, bloody hell," Claire said.

That was an understatement.

My mind raced. "How long do we have before the magical imbalance in the Underworld goes haywire?"

Roarke drew in a breath, debating. "A few days, maybe? It's nearly impossible to say."

"So we have to fix this fast," Aidan said. "Kill as many of the demons as we can to send them back to the Underworld, where their dark magic will restore the balance."

"Which means we need an army." I met Roarke's gaze. "Will the Order of the Magica help us?"

"Of course. But they don't have an army. Fifty mercenaries, tops. Maybe seventy-five if they bring some out of retirement. Then there are about fifty police scattered across the all-magical cities."

There was no standing supernatural army. Our culture just didn't work like that. We weren't big enough for one, and we had enough problems to worry about without starting stupid wars with each other. There were the police to keep civil law in the cities, and a crew of mercenaries and bounty hunters who kept the wayward demons under control.

"I can recruit the Alpha Council," Aidan said. "They will be able to send fighters from among the shifters."

"We can get the League of FireSouls," Nix said.

"And the hellhounds," I added.

"I can recruit the Swamp Supes in the Everglades," Cade said.

"The ones who lived in that village on stilts?" I asked.

"Yeah." He nodded. "They're there because they don't want to be law-abiding citizens, but they also aren't demons or even particularly bad people. They'll fight for this."

Emile raised a hand. Ralph and Rufus stood at attention. "I know some monsters I can recruit. I can use my gift to explain to them what's going on. I think they'd join. Demons like to use them as beasts of burden, and they won't be keen on that."

I nodded gratefully. "Okay, with the Ice Fae, the Order's mercenaries and police, the Alpha Council, the League, the hellhounds, the Swamp Supes, and the monsters, we might have a chance."

"That can't be more than five hundred, though, can it?" Nix asked.

"We'll have to see. We can ask other supernaturals to fight, but not everyone is a warrior." A lot of supernaturals were peaceful, with gifts that didn't relate to fighting at all. "Mordaca and Aerieca might come through with some folks from Darklane."

"Good," Cass said. "Then we need to decide where to attack them."

"Their groups are shifting around too much," Roarke said. "It'd be better to get them all in one place. A setup where we have the upper hand. That way, our numbers won't be as much of an issue."

"So we need to draw them to us," Aidan said. "But how?"

A light bulb went off in my head, bright and strong. "I have an idea. It's crazy, but it could work."

CHAPTER TEN

As it turned out, we didn't even have to visit the League of FireSouls to get their help. As soon as I'd shared my battle plan, Cass, Nix, and I sent a letter with Pond Flower, explaining the situation to the league and asking them to meet us at the battle location. There was no safer way to transport a letter than by hellhound.

The answer had returned almost immediately—an emphatic yes. Even Flora was going to come, though she was still pissed we'd escaped her freezing charm. Relief had made my shoulders sag. Not only did we have their desperately needed help, it also meant Cass, Nix, and I wouldn't have to go recruit help the next day.

I spent the night with Roarke, though by unspoken agreement, we didn't talk about the day to come. All of our friends would be off enlisting aid—and we'd only succeed if everyone we asked agreed to risk their lives for us in the battle the following day.

After the night with Roarke, while everyone was off recruiting help, I met Nix and Cass at P & P. As usual,

Pond Flower followed along. Connor was quick with the coffee as well as the potions. We grabbed a quick bite, then bought three invisibility potions.

Out on the sidewalk, the morning was cold and clear. Oregon was beautiful on days like this.

"Ready?" Cass asked.

"Like a cat's ready for tuna." I called upon my dragon sense, feeding it my desire to find the Shadows. We thought they'd show up at the battle—how could they resist, if we'd gathered all their demons in one place?—but since I was the only one capable of killing them, it'd be best if three didn't attack me at once. That was a recipe for a disastrous death. So we planned to go to them, trying to kill at least one, if not more.

Finally, my dragon sense tugged. "Germany."

Cass's brows rose. "You think they're in that castle where they kept Draka's egg?"

"We're too far away to tell exactly, but I'd bet on it. It was heavily fortified and almost impenetrable. They'd have to let us in—or screw up royally—to allow outsiders to breach the defenses."

"We can make them screw up," Nix said.

At my side, Pond Flower gave a low woof. I glanced down at her, an idea forming in my mind. "I think I know just how to do that."

"How?" Nix asked. "I'd rather plot here and be ready to go as soon as we get there."

"Pond Flower here will be a distraction. The demons' magic and weapons can't hurt her when she surrounds herself with her protective flame. So she'll set up a racket outside the gate, howling to high heaven.

When they come out of the building to stop her, we sneak in through the open gate." I held up the vial of invisibility potion that Connor had given me. "We knew these would come in handy, right?"

They grinned. I looked down at Pond Flower. "You in?"

She gave a low woof. I nodded gratefully.

"I like it," Nix said. "You find the Shadow you want to kill, we'll keep his demon guards off your tail."

"Good plan." Cass held out her hands. "Let's get a move on. I'll take us to the forest about two hundred yards away from the castle. Close to that cave you stayed in with Roarke."

Nix gave a dramatic swoon. "Such a romantic first vacation."

I laughed, punched her lightly in the arm, then grabbed Cass's hand. Nix did the same, and Pond Flower pressed herself against my side.

Cass used her teleportation magic to take us through the ether. We arrived in Germany a moment later. Snow drifted down lightly from the sky. That was good. It could only help our cause, giving us just a bit more camouflage.

"I think we should take the potions now." I uncorked mine.

The others nodded, downing theirs quickly. Almost immediately, they disappeared. I drank the little vial, shuddering at the horrible muddy taste, and waited for the icy magic to flow through my veins. It did, quickly, and soon I could see Cass and Nix.

"Ready?"

They nodded.

"Then let's go." I hurried through the forest, following my dragon sense.

The gray exterior wall loomed out of the distance, and we headed for the heavy gate. I turned to Pond Flower and whispered, "Hide and howl, okay? Be super annoying."

She gave an understanding jerk of her head, then turned and ran into the trees. We crept up to the very edge of the gate, which was a massive iron and wooden affair that would lift vertically into the castle wall when a lever was pulled. We pressed our backs to the stone. I used my gift over ice to call down more snow, enough to cover our tracks and make it hard to see much of anything at all.

As if on cue, Pond Flower set up a racket, howling like a banshee possessed. There was a scuffle from inside the castle walls.

"Wot the bloody 'ell is that racket?" growled a low voice.

"Some kinda mutt." A little wooden door in the gate creaked open. I could just barely make out part of a demon's head as he stuck it through. "I can't see it."

"Shoot it." The demand was grumpy.

I scowled. Jerk.

"I said I can't see it!"

A fist hit flesh. Demons were dumb.

"Well, if you won't shoot it, I will," said the grumpy voice.

Good luck with that.

Another head poked out the little window. I could only see the tips of the demon's horns, which were charred black. Finally, he grumbled, "Damn it, you're right."

"Maybe it'll shut up," said the other demon.

As if she'd heard the words, Pond Flower howled again, giving it an extra dose of something shrieky. It needed to be louder though—something that forced them out of the cabin.

I remembered the Whispa demon I'd killed last week in the bar in Darklane while I'd been collecting powers. That creepy, eyeless bastard had possessed the ability to make or muffle sound. I called on that power, directing toward Pond Flower and envisioning her howls becoming louder and louder.

It worked. Her howls were now so annoying and so loud that it was painful. I flew my hands up to cover my ears, and Nix and Cass did the same. It was the worst noise ever.

The demons definitely agreed, because they groaned.

"Shut that beast up!" a low, sonorous voice drifted across the castle walls.

I shuddered. That was a Shadow, no doubt about it. And he did *not* like Pond Flower.

And the demons didn't like disobeying the Shadow. They rushed to open the gate. From the sound of it, they stumbled over each other and fought to be the one to crank the lever.

Finally, the heavy iron door creaked open, the sound of rusty metal chains shrieking. Pond Flower kept up her racket, but the noise sounded like it was getting farther away. She'd probably led them from the castle, and if they got too close, she could always pull her disappearing trick.

I knew she could take care of herself, especially against two particularly dumb demons, but I knocked on my head anyway.

As the gate rose, I called upon a bit more snow, creating a heavy storm right over the castle. The gate reached its zenith, and the demons hurried through. Immediately, the gate creaked and began lowering. We slipped inside. I was careful to use my ice magic to cover our tracks with snow.

The courtyard looked as I'd remembered it. Large and barren, with demons on the ramparts high above. Fortunately, they were all watching their brethren fail to hunt a hellhound.

Since it was important to get where we would leave no hastily covered tracks in the snow, we raced to the main building where we'd been before. I checked to make sure all the demons' backs were turned—which they were—and cracked open the door so we could slip inside.

As before, the foyer was large and empty. I sagged against the wall, finally breathing properly for the first time since we'd approached the castle. Nix and Cass leaned next to me, panting.

"Give me a moment," I whispered, calling upon my dragon sense.

My *deirfiúr's* magic swelled as they used their own dragon senses.

After a moment, mine tugged in two directions. "Shit. Two of them are somewhere in the labyrinth, I think."

Nix shook her head. "Not interested in going that direction."

"Yeah, we barely made it out last time," Cass said.

"Agreed. Even if we could make it through, we don't have a ton of time. We can't risk getting caught before the battle." I pointed left toward a long hall. "The other Shadow is that way. High up, I think. In a tower."

"Of course he's lurking in a tower," Nix muttered.

"The only other logical option is the dungeons," Cass said with a low laugh. "Bad guys never hang out in normal rooms watching TV."

"True enough. Let's go." I hurried through the empty foyer toward the hallway. It was a warmer space, with wooden floors and silk paneled walls. Upon further inspection, the silk was tattered and moldy and the floors had lost all their sheen, but it was better than the cold stone foyer. That place reminded me of how my parent's castle used to be. Yikes.

We passed by several rooms on silent feet. We were so used to creeping quietly that I didn't even need to use the Whispa demon power to muffle our footsteps. Though we saw no demons, I occasionally felt creepy magical signatures. They were here, guards lurking in corners and behind closed doors. Minions who wouldn't leave their masters' sides.

We reached the base of a wide tower. Spiral stone stairs wound upward. They were wider than most I'd seen—at least five feet across—and it was impossible to tell how many floors up they went. I recalled some fairly large towers, so it could be quite high.

"This way." I crept up the tower stairs, careful to keep my footsteps silent and my ears alert for guards.

We reached a small landing. There might have once been a room here, but now it was empty. We continued onto the next flight of stairs, continuing ever upward. It stayed silent, and the higher we got, the fewer the windows. It was shadowy and dark, very fitting for the Shadow's lair.

I focused on the magic that hung heavy in the air. It prickled against my skin, a familiar warning. There was a protective charm here. My heart raced. Something was happening. But what?

Stones in the walls began to shift, scraping against each other.

"Watch the walls!" I whispered.

"Could be murder holes," Nix said.

We'd seen the horrible things back at the castle in England, ages ago. They'd shot arrows at us, which was totally unwelcome.

But then, the castle had thought the same about us.

As soon as Nix had spoken the words, the stone by my ear emitted the faintest scraping sound. I ducked, moving on instinct. The low shriek of metal sounded over my head. I looked up. A sharp metal spear had shot out of the wall, right where my temple would have been.

I shuddered. "That's a new kind of murder hole."

Nix and Del crouched low, freezing. As long as we stayed still, we wouldn't set off any more of the iron spikes. But that wouldn't get us very far. We needed a way up.

I shifted into my Phantom form, letting the icy magic flow though me. Once I was fully transparent, I reached up to touch the metal spike. It was cold and solid beneath my touch. Shocked, I pressed my palm hard against it. But nothing happened. My hand didn't drift through as it should have while I was a Phantom.

"It looks like they may have been expecting you," Cass whispered.

Nix whistled low. "However they enchanted that, it's a strong magic if it could pierce your Phantom form."

"No kidding." But they were one of the very few types of supernaturals that could hurt me while I was in a Phantom, so it made sense they possessed magic that could do the same. And of course they'd want to protect themselves. They were my number one targets after all the horrible shit they'd done.

Nix's magic swelled, the scent of flowers filling the stairwell. I turned, and she thrust two heavy iron shields at me. "Protect yourself with these."

I hefted them. They were so heavy they made my arms ache, but the spears wouldn't be able to pierce iron this thick. When the metal collided, it'd be loud as hell, though.

We'd need the Whispa demon's power to muffle the sound. No way I wanted demon guards chasing us up these stairs. I called upon it, letting it fill me. It was a difficult power to use and I couldn't be entirely sure that I was doing it correctly, but I envisioned the stairwell becoming completely silent no matter what happened.

"Thanks." The muscles in my arms trembled as I lifted the shields to protect my head and torso and hurried up the stairs.

My *deirfiúr* followed on silent feet. The stones shifted as I ran, but it was fairly quiet. The first spear that struck my shield threw me against the opposite wall. The force was enormous. My shoulder sang with pain where it'd crashed into the stone wall, but I righted myself.

At least the sound was just a dull clang instead of a loud one. Behind me, there was another dull thud, and another. The spears were hitting Nix and Cass's shields as well.

We struggled up the stairs, fighting our way past the battering rams of steel spikes that threw us about. But we were lucky—we made it to the top without being skewered. Bruised, sure. But skewered, no.

I considered it a win.

"That was rough." Nix panted as we hurried across the landing to the next winding flight of stairs. The magic changed here, the signature more of a slimy burn than the prickle that I was used to.

"This is different," I murmured.

"Yeah." Cass lowered her shield. "I don't think it's going to be spikes."

"No, they'd want to keep us on our toes." But I held on to my shield as I crept up the stairs, my senses alert for any change in the magic that might signal what was coming at us.

This time when the stones shifted, it happened below our feet. The stairs right in front of me fell away.

"Shit!" I leapt to the next step.

Nix jumped up behind me, dropping her shields with a clang. In my shock, I'd lost control of the Whispa demon's control over sound. Everything was happening so fast that I didn't have time to pick it back up again.

Cass's magic swelled behind me, but I didn't turn to look. I raced up the stairs.

It took only a second for the stairs to fall away once I stepped on them, sometimes less. I had to be fast if my *deirfiúr* were going to be able to run up to safety behind me. I shifted back to human form, hoping to give Nix something solid to grab onto if she fell. We sprinted up the stairs, barely keeping ahead of the disappearing stairs.

Beside me, an enormous spider scuttled along the wall. An involuntary shriek escaped me as it brushed past. I cringed away, then glanced frantically behind to make sure Cass and Nix were okay.

Cass was gone.

"The spider is Cass!" Nix said, eyes wide.

Cass had shifted into an animal form

Go, Cass.

Nix and I raced upwards. We were almost to the top when the step beneath me fell away too soon. I fell, scrabbling to catch the stair in front of me. I gripped it with my fingertips as Nix grabbed onto me from behind. There was nothing but air beneath my feet. My muscles burned.

I held us aloft, just barely. If I could just scramble up...

The stair that I clung to dropped away entirely. We plummeted. My heart leapt into my throat. Something caught us hard. A sticky net of some kind. We yanked to a stop, dangling in the stairwell, and bumping against the wall.

Panic beat in my chest. Had the Shadows caught us?

The stones whirled around us as we spun in our trap, caught up in a net that began to hoist us up the now-hollow stairwell. I looked up to see what had trapped us and saw the back of an enormous spider on the ceiling.

I nearly shrieked, unable to help myself. I did *not* like spiders, even if they were family. This one was even bigger than Cass's first attempt at shifting into an arachnid.

But it was still her. I drew in a ragged breath. It had to be. There couldn't be that many altruistic giant spiders in a murderer's castle. She must have shifted again, knowing she'd need to be bigger to save us.

Slowly, she hauled us up to the landing, performing a feat of spider strength that wowed me. Truthfully, I had no idea how strong spiders were, but Cass's magic was seriously impressive.

Nix and I tumbled onto the stone floor, trapped in her webbing.

"Ew, ew, ew." Now that we were safe, I was desperate to escape the sticky web. I drew my sword from the ether, slicing free from my side of the net, while Nix conjured a dagger and cut herself out.

We rolled away from the web, batting it away from our bodies. My skin crawled as I tore the sticky stuff off.

"If I didn't have such high self-esteem, I'd think you didn't like me in my spider form," Cass said.

Gasping, I spun to see her leaning against the wall, grinning.

Normally, she had to be near Aidan to use her Mirror Mage powers to copy his ability to shift into any animal, but she could also store up a bit of his gift to use later if she wanted. She'd probably blown it all in that one show, but it'd been...

"That was *amazing*." I held up my hand for a high five. "Gross, but amazing."

"Seconded." Nix tore some web from her hair. "But we need to get a move on. We've been loud as hell, and there's no way that there aren't guards on the way."

"Right." I called upon the Whispa demon's power again, muffling sound and hoping that if we were quiet as we climbed, they'd think we'd fallen and died in their stair trap.

I hurried toward the stairs, pulling to a stop as soon as I reached them. What fresh hell would this flight bring? I prayed we were near the top.

Fortunately, it was a challenge that I was up for. We'd only traveled five stairs when a noise sounded from above. I jumped back just as a heavy iron gate slammed down. It was quiet, but still shocking.

"Wow, this guy is ready for intruders," I muttered.

"That's a serious gate," Nix said. "Del, you could drift through in Phantom form, Cass could crawl through as a mouse, but I'm stuck."

"Not for long." No way was I leaving Nix behind. Splitting up was a terrible idea. "Step down a few stairs."

They obeyed, retreating. I reached out and called on my iron magic, touching the metal with my palm and envisioning it melting in a puddle. It worked quickly, the metal turning bright red, then orange, before dripping down to the floor.

I stood toward the side, making sure it didn't melt through my boots. Once I'd created a hole big enough to pass through, I pulled away. I gave the metal a moment to stop actively dripping, then I jumped over the pile of molten metal and hurried up the stairs.

Nix and Cass followed. Two more iron gates stopped us, but I melted them both.

By the time we reached the top, the sound of pounding footsteps sounded from below.

"Looks like they've figured out we're here," I said.

Fortunately, we'd reached a heavy wooden and iron door. This had to be the Shadow's lair. My dragon sense confirmed it, pulling hard toward the door.

"You get the Shadow. We'll get your back," Nix said.

"Good luck," Cass said.

"Thanks." As the footsteps pounded ever upward, I shifted into my Phantom form and tried to drift through the door.

The metal straps on the wooden door stopped me, however. They were enchanted with whatever had made the iron spikes so dangerous. Damn it.

We didn't have time for delays.

We also didn't have a choice.

I reached out, using my iron magic to melt the metal. Once it was gone, I waved goodbye to my *deirfiúr*. They were no longer looking at me. Instead, they'd taken up battle positions, Nix with a sword and Cass with her magical flame hovering around her hand.

I turned back and drifted through the door, dodging a hard left as soon as I'd made it through. Something heavy thudded into the door, piercing it like a fork into steak.

An iron spike—just like the ones from down below.

The Shadow who'd hurled it was on the other side of the room, waiting for me to enter. His dark cloak floated around him, like he was the Grim Reaper underwater. Malevolence drifted off him, a feeling that was impossible to ignore.

The Shadow threw another enchanted spear. It hurtled through the air, and I barely dodged in time, throwing myself farther left, behind a heavy wooden chair.

My heart raced as I took stock of my situation.

Throwing enchanted metal bolts was this Shadow's magical gift. Which explained how they'd gotten the rare magic to enchant the spikes that could hurt a Phantom. He'd made them. I scrambled along the floor as he threw his iron bolts, one after the other.

So far, this wasn't going well for me. I was scuttling about like a frightened rat. I needed to get it together and use some of the magical arsenal I'd collected over the last couple weeks. There was no other way I'd get close enough to kill this bastard before he skewered me like a kebab.

Frantic, I called upon my telekinesis, envisioning hurling a table at him. The heavy wooden table against the far window shot across the room, flying through the Shadow. It didn't hurt him—only I could do that—but it startled him. He couldn't see through a table, after all.

"Weren't expecting that, were you?" I said.

He just hissed, throwing spear after spear toward me.

One after the other, I threw every piece of furniture in the room at him. Once it'd all splintered against the stone walls, I moved on to the tapestries. They obscured his vision even better. All the while, I crept closer, drawing my sword from the ether as I got within striking distance.

Finally, I was near enough that I could attack. I swept out with my blade, slicing his legs. As he toppled, I leapt to my feet and lunged for him, sinking my blade into his stomach.

With the last of his strength, he hurled an iron spear at me. I dodged, but not well enough. It didn't skewer me, but it took a chunk out of my upper arm as it flew past.

Pain flared through me, burning and hot. I ignored it in favor of sinking my blade through his throat, finishing the job.

His shadowy form collapsed.

Dead.

The door behind me exploded in a ball of flame. The heat seared my back and I whirled, blade raised. Nix and Cass hurtled in, panting and wild-eyed.

"You done?" Nix demanded.

"Yep!"

"Let's go, then!" Cass raced for me, Nix at her heels. We collided together, clutching each other close. Cass called on her teleportation magic and zapped us out of there, taking us back to Ancient Magic.

Pond Flower sat on the stoop, grinning at us with her tongue lolling out.

Later that night, after saying goodbye to Nix and Cass and letting Aidan heal my wounded arm, I sat in my apartment with Pond Flower, waiting for Roarke to arrive. Pond Flower was curled up on the couch, way too big for it.

Roarke knocked on my apartment door. I knew it was him without even opening it. I could just barely smell the sandalwood scent of his magic. Pond Flower stayed on the couch, entirely uninterested in Roarke.

I'd insisted we spend the night here. I didn't want to be too far from my *deirfiúr* the night before the battle that could signal my ultimate defeat.

I pulled open the door, grinning at the sight of Roarke. He wore dark jeans and a black sweater. The whole effect somehow made him even more attractive, with his black hair and eyes and killer body.

"Hey." I gestured him inside.

He stepped in, pulling me forward for a kiss. When his lips pressed to mine, my heartbeat thundered. I reached up and wrapped my arms around his neck, taking the kiss deeper.

Instead of kissing me more, though, he groaned and pulled away.

"Hang on," he said. "I want to make sure this place is safe for the night."

"You mean, in case the Shadows send their demons after me again?"

"Exactly. I know you said that your apartments were well warded against break-ins, but you should have an escape route in case they do manage to make it in."

I gestured to the living room windows, which looked out on the main street, right over Ancient Magic and into the park. "There's those."

"That could work. I've stationed guard demons on the street, just in case. And in the alley near your bedroom."

"Really?" My heart warmed as I walked over to the windows and looked down. A line of demons loitered on the sidewalk, trying to look non-threatening in case the cops showed up. Demons shouldn't really be hanging around like that—especially since most people were like I had been and didn't realize that there were actually quite a few good demons out there. Fortunately, these guys didn't look super intimidating.

"Is there a back entrance?" Roarke asked. "To the alley out back?"

There was, through the windows in my trove.

I glanced at him, suddenly wondering if he knew about my trove. I'd never told him, though he might know that FireSouls had troves. We were dragons after all. Sort of, at least.

I suddenly felt compelled to share it all with him. It was important to me, after all. And so was he.

"There is." I started toward the bedroom and gestured for him to follow. "Come on, there's something I want to show you."

I led him back and stood in front of the empty wall to my trove. Normally I'd just walk through in Phantom form, but he wouldn't be able to follow if I did that. So I pressed my hand to the wall and fed it my magic. A door appeared, and I opened it, then stepped inside.

I flicked on the lights as he entered. His eyes widened.

"This is…" He searched for words. "Impressive."

"Thanks."

"It's your trove?"

I nodded. "So you knew about them? That FireSouls have them?"

He slowly wandered into the space, careful not to knock over any piles of books. "I do. Once you told me what you were, I did more research. There isn't much about your kind, but I did learn about this."

"Yet you never asked to see it?"

He turned to me, the understanding and love in his gaze so clear. I stepped back, startled.

"You're always wary, Del. Understandably. You don't need me pushing you for more. I was content to wait." He smiled. "You needed me to wait. I knew it wouldn't be forever, so I did. But damn, I wanted you to tell me."

And that was why I loved him. Among the many other reasons why—his kindness, intelligence, and strength—he cared about me more than himself.

It was obvious now—I loved Roarke.

That was crazy. But it was true. I'd barely known him two months, but it was now so obvious to me that we'd spend the rest of our lives together.

How had I not realized it sooner? It felt like I should have known it the moment he'd walked into Ancient Magic, intent on dragging me back to the Underworld.

I walked to him and wrapped my arms around his neck, leaning up to kiss him. I pressed my lips to his, just briefly, then pulled away. "You're the best man I've ever met."

The corner of his mouth cocked up in a smile so charming that it made my heart race. "I don't know if I'd say that."

I laughed softly. "Well, I would. And I love you."

Joy spread across his face, warming his eyes. "About time."

I laughed.

"I've loved you forever, I think," Roarke said. "Since well before this moment."

"Really? And you didn't say anything?"

He shrugged, looping his arms around my waist and pulling me closer. "Didn't want to scare you off."

I smiled. "Impossible."

"I know that now." He picked me up, sweeping me into his arms, and carried me to the couch in the middle of the trove.

"There are windows in the back of the trove that lead to the alley?" he asked as he walked.

"Yes."

"Good. I've already stationed demons out there anyway. We should be safe."

"Thank you."

He sat on the couch, and I curled up next to him. My heart felt so full all of a sudden. I had my *deirfiúr*, my other friends, and now Roarke. I had everything. I just had to make sure I kept it.

It was vital that we win tomorrow, for so many reasons. Now that I'd found Roarke—found love—I didn't want to lose it.

"So this means you'll move in with me?" Roarke asked.

I lay my head on his shoulder. "You don't mind being pushy about that, do you?"

"No." He wrapped an arm around me. "Not now that you've confessed to loving me."

"I guess I did, didn't I?" I leaned up and kissed his neck.

"Oh, you did."

"Then okay, I'll move in with you. Half-time. The other time, we're here." It was the perfect solution.

He smiled. "I can live with that. Compromise."

"Oh, and I have a dog."

"I'm okay with that." He glanced down at me, his dark gaze wry. "Though I'm not sure I'd call Pond Flower a dog."

"She's certainly not a regular dog. But she's mine." I looked around at the trove, at the piles of books and lucky charms. "You really don't think this place is too weird? I'm basically a hoarder."

"Oh, it's weird."

I punched him in the shoulder.

He grinned down at me. "Good weird, though."

With that, he leaned down and kissed me. I wrapped my arms around him and sank into the kiss, welcoming his touch. If this was the way I was going to spend what might be my last night on Earth, I was totally okay with it.

CHAPTER ELEVEN

The next day, I stood on a massive platform overlooking the battle preparations. We'd chosen a valley between the mountains in Kamchatka, not too far from where the Ice Fae made their home.

We were far enough that their village wouldn't take another hit, but being so close to the source of their power gave them an advantage. And hopefully the cold would slow the unprepared demons. Many of the Underworlds were hot and they wouldn't fare well in this biting cold.

The area we'd selected was shaped like a bowl between the mountains. The battlefield would take place on the tundra, but most of our allies were waiting in the mountains, ready to attack from behind.

I'd arrived at dawn, along with Cass, Nix, Roarke, and Aidan. We'd used magic to build a tall platform smack in the middle of the valley. It would be the center of attention for the demons.

The platform was forty feet tall and the size of a basketball court. The sides were vertical and slicked down with ice provided by the Ice Fae, making it almost impossible for demons to climb.

"The League of FireSouls look like they're coming along well." Nix pointed to the four impenetrable forts that they'd built out in the battlefield. The bunkers were positioned roughly at north, south, east, and west, and were only about thirty yards from the base of our platform.

"They do."

The little buildings were built of stone that would repel magic. From inside, our fighters would launch potion bombs meant to take out as many demons as possible early on in the fight. The material it took to build the bunkers was ridiculously rare, so they were small and couldn't fit many people, but they'd be useful in defending the platform.

"It's almost time," Roarke said from beside me.

I glanced at the sun, which was now high overhead. Everyone was supposed to be in position by noon. We'd start shortly thereafter.

"Hey, look who came through." Cass pointed down into the mostly empty battlefield.

Aerdeca and Mordaca sauntered across the snowy tundra, straight toward us. Each wore closely fitting military snow gear in their usual colors of white and black. Tactical and practical.

Mordaca's bow was strapped to her back, and Aerdeca had a sword sheathed at her side. When they reached the base, they waved imperiously, no doubt expecting a pickup.

Cade obliged, shifting into his demon form and flying down to pick them up. He wrapped an arm around each woman's waist and brought them up to stand right in front of me.

"So this is the big fight?" Aerdeca looked around.

"Should be," I said.

"We've brought a hundred and thirteen fighters from Darklane. All species." Mordaca pointed to the mountains in the west. "They are waiting there, in the shadows of the rock. At your signal, we will attack."

"You're sure about this?" I asked, hating having to ask anyone to face their death. "Our odds aren't great."

"We're fine with that," Mordaca said.

"And don't underestimate us." Aerdeca arched a pale brow. "Or yourself."

I grinned at her, warmed by her words. "Thanks. The demons will show up, likely in a steady stream. It could take minutes, or hours. I don't know. But their attention will be focused on the platform." *On me.* "Wait for the signal, then you're free to attack."

Aerdeca gave a wicked grin, her red lips curling. I shivered, glad I wasn't a demon she would soon set her sights on.

"See you when it's over." Aerdeca turned and walked to the edge of the platform.

"You've got this," Mordaca said. "If we didn't believe it, we wouldn't be here."

"Wow, thanks." I searched for the right words. "That's really sweet."

"Don't tell Queen Bitch." She nodded back to Aerdeca, who was gazing impatiently at her. "I've got a reputation to uphold."

She winked, then joined Aerdeca.

Good friends came in strange packages, it seemed. Cade flew them down to the ground. I turned to Roarke. "The mercenaries will be here, right?"

He nodded. "Sixty-five of them, plus fifty police officers. They'll attack from the north, along with Emile and his monsters."

"Perfect." That covered all the sides of the compass. Mordaca and Aerdeca leading the Darklaners from the west, the Ice Fae attacking from the east, and the Shifters from the south. Those with wings would take to the air. The Swamp Supes—ninety of which had agreed to come—would do whatever the hell they wanted, and I was grateful for it. I wasn't about to turn down help of any variety.

The hellhounds, who couldn't be hurt while they deployed their protective black flame, would stay on the ground, guarding the FireSouls who would go directly into the middle of the fray once their bombs had been deployed.

My friends would be up here with me. Because even though the platform was raised, the demons would still manage to attack it. If not from the air, then with magic. Unfortunately, our plan made it so that hiding behind a protective barrier was impossible.

"I wish Draka and the other Phantom dragons would arrive," I said, worry eating at my insides. "I know she'll show. She always does. But I'd like her to show *now.*"

Roarke wrapped an arm around my shoulders and squeezed.

We watched the FireSouls put the finishing touches on the bunkers. Aidan gave directions, as he was the one who had obtained the special material to build them and knew best how to use it. It was something his security company was working on. We were lucky to have the hookup.

No matter how prepared we were, I couldn't shake my nerves. This was going to be one hell of a fight.

Finally, the bunkers were done. The sun was near its zenith.

On the ground, Aidan shifted into his griffin form. He was massive, his golden fur and wings shining in the sun. Alton and Corin, my two favorite FireSouls, climbed onto his back. He lunged into the air, his massive wings carrying them gracefully toward us.

When he landed lightly on the platform, Alton and Corin climbed down. They both wore the burnished red leather armor of the FireSouls, with their swords strapped into sheathes and ready to use.

"You're sure about this?" I asked. "Those bunkers are safe, but nothing is guaranteed."

Corin grinned. "As if I planned to stay in the bunker anyway." She patted the handle of one of the swords strapped over her back. "I prefer to fight with these. Once I've hurled as many potion bombs as I've been given, I'm getting out of that stone box and onto the battlefield."

Alton gave her a warning look. "Stay in the bunker until all the bombs are thrown."

"Yeah, yeah." She punched him lightly on the shoulder.

But Alton's advice was good. The potion bombs we'd brought were *strong*. They were our heavy hitters, and we'd open with them before anyone on our side went onto the battlefield.

"Thank you for coming," I said.

"We wouldn't be anywhere else," Alton said. "It's our sworn duty to help you and the rest of the Triumvirate." He swept a hand out to indicate the battlefield and our many soldiers camped in the mountains beyond. "This is clearly the end of your task. We must help you succeed."

I drew in a ragged breath, grateful to have their support while being simultaneously terrified that I'd let everyone down.

But crippling fear would get me nowhere, so I stashed it and stuck out my hand. Alton took it, giving two strong shakes, but Corin hugged me before stepping back.

She glanced at Aidan, who was still in griffin form. "Can we get another ride?"

He walked to them and knelt. They climbed on, and he had them delivered safely to the ground a moment later.

It was the last safe thing they would do all day.

While we waited for the all-good signals from the various factions, it began to snow lightly.

"I'm not sure if this is a good sign or a bad one," I said.

"We'll find out soon enough." Roarke squeezed my hand.

A flare shot off in the distance, from the mountains to the north, rising bright and orange into the sky. Emile and his monsters were ready, along with the Order's mercenaries and police. A moment later, the Darklaners in the west shot off their flare. From the south, the Shifters fired a flare, and from the east, the Ice Fae launched theirs. Corin stood on top of her bunker and waved. And lastly, Cade flew up from the mountains in the northeast, a dark bullet in the sky that signaled the Swamp Supes were ready to fight.

"This is it." I looked around at my friends.

Roarke, Nix, Cass, Aidan, Connor, and Claire all stood with me on the platform. They'd have my back while I...

Was bait.

Nix hoisted her bow. "We've got this."

"It's nothing," Cass said. "Just a regular day."

"I, personally, have been wanting a decent fight," Claire said.

"Same," Connor said. "Baking bread has been getting old. I have some potion bombs I've been dying to try out."

Aidan, who was still in his griffin form, grinned at me. At least, I thought it was a grin. I was grateful for his help. He'd been a good ally ever since he'd hooked up with Cass.

Roarke reached for my hand. I gripped his.

It was obvious what my friends were doing, and I appreciated it. I was already nervous as hell that a lot of great people were about to die. Lightening the mood helped, if only a little bit.

"Thank you, guys."

"Always," Cass and Nix said in unison.

"Let's get to work." Claire picked up her bag of potion bombs that had been made by Connor. "I've got a date tonight."

She winked, then turned to take up her position on the east side of the platform. Her brother joined her, while Cass and Nix took the west, and Aidan took the north.

Roarke reached for me, pulling me toward him and pressing a kiss to my lips.

"You can do this," he said.

I kept my gaze glued to his. "Thanks."

I kissed him one last time, then pushed him away. He shifted into his demon form, suddenly much taller and scarier than he had been, and walked to his side of the platform. I turned to the amplifier stone. The shining black obsidian gleamed as snowflakes landed on its surface.

I knocked on my head for good luck, then adopted my Phantom form and lay my hand upon the cool black glass, calling upon my magic.

Who would have guessed that the Ubilaz demon's power would end up saving the day?

Possibly.

We still had to kill all the demons who showed up.

It took me a while to access the magic. After I'd learned to control it, I'd shoved it so far down inside of me that I'd almost forgotten I had it. Who in their right mind would want to attract murderous demons to them? Every time those demons had followed the Ubilaz demon's call and realized that it was me instead of their number one fave, they'd wanted to kill me.

But we needed a way to get all the demons in one place. And this was the perfect way. The Ubilaz demon's magic called to them like catnip. Just being near an Ubilaz gave other demons a high that was worth traveling for.

Finally, the magic sparked to life inside of me. I drew on it, envisioning every evil demon in the world showing up in this valley. It thrummed inside my chest, eager to be set free.

So I let it have its way, feeding it into the amplifying stone. The enchanted obsidian would send the magic out stronger and farther. It was the reason we hadn't built protective walls around the platform—we didn't want anything interfering with the magic that should attract the demons to us.

When the first demons appeared on the battlefield, relief and fear collided in my chest. It had worked!

More and more demons appeared. Dozens at a time. Their gazes immediately riveted to me on the platform. At first, there was confusion on their faces. I couldn't blame them. I sure as heck didn't look like an Ubilaz demon. But then there was annoyance, and rage. Yep, they knew something was up.

And they were pissed about it.

From the shouts below, I assumed there were many more demons on the ground right below the platform.

I wanted to yank my hand off the stone and grab up one of Connor's potion bombs to hurl it at the demons who continued to arrive on the battlefield.

"It's working!" Nix shouted. "Keep going, Del!"

She was right. I couldn't join the fight yet. I had to keep doing this, calling as many evil demons as I could. It'd take them time to appear. Not all had the power of teleportation or could hitch a ride with a friend who had it. Many would have to use transportation charms and other means of magical transportation.

But they were arriving quickly. More and more, until there were hundreds surging toward the platform to get to me. I'd be lying if I said it didn't make me nervous. Many of them had probably used their last transportation charms to get to me, so they were pissed. Add to that their annoyance at not getting their Ubilaz demon contact high, they'd want my blood.

Fortunately, my friends were here to fight when I couldn't.

Our first wave of attack began once the field was crowded enough. The FireSouls in the bunkers hurled their potion bombs from the tiny windows. They flew through the air, brilliant green liquid inside of a round glass vial. As soon as they landed in the midst of a crowd of demons, they exploded on impact.

The sound was deafening, making my ears ring as green flame and smoke shot into the air. Demon bodies flew in all direction. Each bomb had to take out a dozen, maybe two. But more demons appeared every second.

Nix fired her arrows straight down against the wall of the platform, undoubtedly firing on the demons who tried to climb the ice wall. Cass hurled fireballs, while Connor and Claire threw potion bombs that were slightly smaller—ideal for taking out nearby demons without toppling our platform. I couldn't see their hits landing, but I could hear the shouts of the demons.

No doubt some would realize this wasn't worth it and leave, but we'd banked on demon nature—most would stay for the fight. And when they died, they'd end up back in the Underworld. Trapped.

"You're doing great!" Cass called to me.

I grinned weakly, but I wasn't feeling particularly great. My muscles were trembling with the strain of using so much magic, but I couldn't stop until the demons quit appearing.

Eventually, the other two Shadows would probably show. Part of me wanted them to so we could get this over with. But the smart part of me knew it would be best to save that fight for another day, when we weren't distracted by two thousand demons. There were now at least that many in the field, with more arriving every moment.

Beside me, Roarke and Aidan launched themselves into the sky. I glanced up, seeing that winged demons had arrived, staging an attack from the air. From the south, flying shifters hurtled toward their foes. Most of them were massive birds of prey, but there were a few mythological figures as well.

From below, the FireSoul bunkers each shot off a purple flare. They were out of bombs. It was safe for the fighters in the mountains to launch their attack from behind.

Once all four bunkers had shot off their flares, the trapdoors in the tops of the little buildings burst open. The FireSouls climbed out, followed by their hellhound guards. Pond Flower stuck close by Corin, for which I was grateful.

"Launch the last flare!" I yelled.

Connor pulled it out of his back pocket and lit it, shooting it into the sky. The bright orange light signaled that the battle was about to change.

In the distance all around, fighters flowed out of the mountains and across the plains. There were no war whoops or shouts as they ran. They were the element of surprise, pinning our demon enemies against the tower.

Within minutes, they were at the backs of the demons. Their pounding footsteps eventually alerted our foe, who turned to face them. From the east, the Ice Fae shot their freezing magic, turning the demons into popsicles that toppled to the ground. With their blood frozen and their hearts stopped, they'd die within moments.

From the west, Mordaca and Aerdeca raced across the field. Mordaca fired arrows from her bow as quickly as a professional archer. Around her, Darklaners of various talents hurled their magical weapons. Flame, lightning, sonic booms, and jets of ice felled the demons on their side of the valley.

I wanted to get into the fight so badly I could taste it. But demons were still appearing, dozens at a time. And we weren't yet outmanned because of our superior planning and the element of surprise, so I should keep calling them.

We had one chance, and I couldn't screw it up.

I fed more magic into the amplifier stone as the battle raged around me. Above, Aidan, Roarke, and the flying shifters kept the winged demons from reaching me. My friends on the platforms fired their weapons into the demons down below.

In the distance, Emile led the monsters into battle. He rode a massive two-headed dog who thundered across the tundra. Though he was too far away for me to see Ralph and Rufus, I knew that they rode on his shoulders, whiskers twitching in the wind. Before the battle, Emile had told me that the dog's name was Prince Louie—Prince was the left head and Louie the right—and that the animal's primary power was killing with his poison breath. Behind Emile, giant winged snakes, the massive red demon crabs, huge hounds, and other strange beasts raced for the demons.

The Swamp Supes flowed into the valley from all sides. There was no Skunk Ape, though I'd have liked to have seen him. The battle raged around us as the smell of a thousand different magical signatures filled the air.

Finally, the demons stopped arriving. Nearly all evil demons on Earth were here, right now. The battlefield was full. Bodies piled everywhere. Most were the enemy, for which I was grateful. So far, our plan was working.

I removed my hand from the stone at the same time demons began to climb onto the platform.

I drew my sword from the ether and hurried to the edge, joining Nix, who fired at any demon climbing onto our turf. Once I was close enough to see clearly, I realized that the demons had piled up on top of each other, so many of them that they'd created a mountain of bodies to scramble over.

Shit.

I fired up my ice power, piercing demon after demon through the chest. Cass hurled her flame, barbecuing them until the air smelled disgustingly of burnt demon flesh. Claire had given up on the potion bombs, instead choosing to draw her sword and go at it the old-fashioned way. She lunged and swiped, so graceful that it looked like she was dancing.

Soon, I was sweating from using so much magic, but we weren't making any real headway. Though our fighters from the mountain were slaying demon after demon, there were just too many of them. And they were so intent on getting to me that they continued to pile up to reach me.

Fortunately, this meant that they weren't putting up much of a fight against the supernaturals who attacked them from behind.

Unfortunately, there were so many of them that they were now overrunning the platform. Nix, Cass, Connor, Claire, and I were forced into the middle as demons surrounded us.

"What do we do?" Connor asked.

Sweat broke out on my skin and my hearth thundered. The demons were all species—huge muscular ones who looked like they wanted to rip our heads off and slender, tiny ones who stank of strong, dark magic.

Roarke and Aidan were still busy in the sky, keeping demons from landing straight on our heads, and we were outnumbered here. Despite our ice and flame and arrows and potion bombs, my friends and I were being overrun.

"Hang on," Nix said.

She conjured a brick wall that surrounded us, but demons beat against it, sending cracks through the mortar. Eventually, it tumbled, a pile of brick that was soon crushed under their feet.

Her eyes flashing with desperation, Cass used her gift over fire to build a wall of flame around us. It flickered orange and bright. The heat burned, searing my skin, but some of the demons were able to pass right through.

"Draka!" I screamed.

If we'd ever needed backup, now was the time.

A massive demon lunged for me, reaching out with vicious claws. I powered up an icicle and hurled it at him. The thing plunged into his chest just as he reached me. The demon's gaping mouth revealed a row of double fangs as he sailed through my Phantom form.

I turned just in time to see a demon lunge for Nix's back. I turned corporeal and swiped out with my sword, slicing him through the leg. He fell, still reaching out for Nix. Connor hurled an acid bomb at him and he screamed, stumbling back into the crowd of demons.

Somehow, the demons had destroyed Cass's wall of flame. They were now only inches from us all, so close I could see the pores in their skin.

"Draka!" I screamed.

An answering screech sent joy streaking through me. I looked up to see Draka, her massive blue body sweeping down from the sky. Beside her were the other three Phantom dragons. They plunged into the crowd of demons that surrounded us, scattering them.

Claire whirled with her sword, cutting down the demons that remained. Connor continued to hurl acid bombs, and I shot my icicles. Roarke and Aidan swooped down from the sky, yanking the climbing demons away from the platform. Cade joined them, and Emile charged Prince Louie up to the platform.

The two-headed dog—strangely, one head was a white poodle and the other some kind of golden retriever—opened its jaws and breathed smoky green breath onto a pile of demons who were attempting to reach me. The demons shrieked and writhed, toppling to the ground as the poison killed them. Fortunately, the green breath didn't waft over me.

All the while, Prince Louie's tail wagged like mad. Apparently, he enjoyed a good demon killing.

The tide was turning. The platform was almost free of demons, and Roarke and Aidan were taking care of those that breached our defenses.

But then my gaze caught on a sight that sent ice through my veins.

The Shadows.

They drifted across the field, their dark gray forms cutting a path through the mass of fighting bodies like they were a couple of Moseses parting the Red Sea.

"Incoming," I said.

"I see them." Nix fired an arrow straight at the first Shadow. As expected it flew through him, doing no damage.

Cass blasted a demon with a fire jet, then shouted over her shoulder, "We'll try to hold one off while you take care of the first. Then you can do the last."

"Connor and I will keep the demons off your back." Claire stabbed a red demon through the gut. "And don't forget Roarke and Aidan will take care of the sky."

As I waited for the Shadow to reach the platform, I plowed an icicle through the chest of a slender gray demon with huge horns and fangs like a saber-toothed tiger. "Thanks guys."

It was the last thing I had a chance to say. The first Shadow was on the platform a moment later, having quickly climbed over the pile of demons that Roarke and Aidan were steadily decimating.

The Shadow drifted right toward me, his dark cloak drifting in the wind. The world grew silent around me. Though the battle continued to rage, I heard nothing and felt only the malevolence radiating from the Shadow drifting toward me.

"Looking for me?" I walked backward toward the other side of the platform, drawing the Shadow away from my friends. Emile and Prince Louie were stationed at the base of this side, taking care of any demons who might try to come for my back.

"I would think that is obvious." The Shadow's voice was a sibilant hiss.

I grinned, though my insides were actually churning, and held my sword out in front of me. Slowly, he drew his own blade. It was made of black shadow, the only one of its kind that I had ever seen.

"That's a nice sword," I said. "But I'm going to take it from you."

The Shadow hissed.

Behind him, the other Shadow climbed onto the platform. Cass raced to the amplifying stone, Nix at her side. Cass lay her hand on the stone, then thrust out her palm and created a wall of pure white flame between us and the second Shadow. The Shadow tried to pass through it, but the stone had created some kind of super strong flame that he couldn't cross.

Quick thinking, Cass.

The trapped Shadow raised a hand and flicked out a small tentacle of pure electricity, clearly testing the strength of the fire. It darted through the fire, creating a small hole.

Shit.

As my Shadow slowly drifted toward me, Nix conjured a gleaming golden shield, taking up her position in front of Cass, who kept feeding her magic to the wall of flame. If she took her hand off the amplifier stone, her magic flame would lose its enhancement, and the Shadow could break through.

Their Shadow sent out a whip of electricity. Nix thrust out her shield, ducking her head. The electricity collided with it, sounding like a hammer beating a tin drum, and Nix shook from the force. A rotten scent filled the air.

Poison? Was the Shadow's whip made of electricity and poison? Whatever it was, it was deadly. We couldn't let it touch us.

Together, she and Cass held off the Shadow as he slowly broke down the magical flame. Around us, Connor and Claire fought the other demons.

The Shadow who watched me finally lunged, his blade outstretched. He was fast as a snake. I barely managed to get my own sword up in time. Our blades clashed, the magical metals clanging. A shiver went up my arm, as if his blade imparted a poison to my own.

I whirled away, ducking as he swiped out for me.

"Is this how you thought your plan would go down?" I taunted.

Rage drifted off him, a distinct feeling on the air that made me pray he wouldn't be able to use it against me.

"You traitorous bitch," he growled.

"At your service." I slashed out with my blade, slicing his cloak. He hissed in pain and jerked back, but was quick to recover.

Behind him, the other Shadow was breaking down the flame wall, his gaze intent on me. Every time he lashed a whip of electricity at Nix, she appeared to weaken. But she and Cass held strong, giving me time to defeat the Shadow with the blade.

He whirled, his cloak obscuring his movements, and darted right, catching me by surprise. I fended off his blow, but the next strike landed. His sword swiped over my arm, sending pain flaring through my bicep.

At least it wasn't my sword arm. I darted for him, sinking my sword into his side. He shrieked, but didn't go down. Somehow, he moved faster.

Fear chilled my skin. I couldn't beat this Shadow. He was a better swordsman than me, faster and stronger. As if proving my point, he darted toward me and sliced his blade across my upper thigh. The cut was so deep that I stumbled, blood pouring out of the wound.

I tried to right myself, but was slow and clumsy. My leg could barely hold my weight.

Now I truly couldn't beat this Shadow. It was only a matter of time before he finished me.

Cold sweat broke out all over my body.

I need help.

As if she'd heard my plea, Pond Flower appeared right behind the Shadow, just inches from the back of his legs. Her red eyes gleamed as she stared hard at me.

Taking her cue, I threw myself at my enemy. I stumbled on my injured leg, but it worked. The threat of my oncoming blade made the Shadow step back. He tripped over Pond Flower, whose protective black flame made the Shadow hiss in pain.

I leapt onto him, clumsily straddling him as my weakened leg slowed me down. I thrust my sword through his chest. Viciously, I twisted the blade.

The evil life force that propelled him disappeared almost immediately.

Dead.

One down, one to go. I stood, my wound still pouring blood, and looked toward my *deirfiúr*.

At that moment, the Shadow broke through the enhanced flame barrier. The fire fizzled and disappeared, leaving us open to his attack. He didn't spare a glance for Nix or Cass. Instead, he shot his electric whip out at me. It glowed brilliant white and was thick as a telephone pole.

Without having to feel it, I knew the strike would be deadly. Even in my Phantom form. And with my wound, I was too slow to save myself. Pond Flower turned, as if to throw herself between me and the electric whip, but Nix was faster.

She lunged between me and the weapon, taking the hit full-on. Her shield was no good, and his electricity wrapped around her like a snake.

Horror opened a chasm in my chest as I watched it light her up. Strength that I shouldn't have had welled within me and I charged, slicing through the electric cable with my Phantom blade. Nix dropped to the ground.

Before the Shadow could recover, I lunged for him, flying across the platform on pure adrenaline and rage. I sunk the blade through his chest, then kicked him in the stomach, dislodging him from my sword.

As he fell, I could feel the life force drift out of him. He collapsed like a rag doll. He was dead.

I whirled and raced for Nix, who lay on the ground, broken. Cass was beside her, tears streaming down her cheeks. Nix's face was pale and her fingertips burned. Darkness spread up her arms like ash, slowly creeping toward her face.

Was it the poison from the Shadow's electric whip?

I crashed to my knees beside her.

"Nix!" Tears poured down my face. Pain like I'd never felt tore through me, the claws of a giant tiger.

Nix's eyes fluttered open, a duller green than I'd ever seen.

Draka landed beside us, shifting into her human form. She knelt, touching Nix, then looked up at me, sadness on her timeless face. "Poison. She will die."

No. An icy wasteland opened up inside my chest. I leaned over Nix, weeping.

"Do you know what you did?" I cried.

"Of course." Nix coughed. The black ash traveled up her shoulders, to her neck. "I love you. Del. Cass."

I wanted to squeeze her, to shake her, to force her to heal. But I could do none of it.

"Aidan!" Cass screamed. Calling for his healing powers.

I looked at Draka and begged, "Heal her."

"I don't have that power." Sadness was a mask over her normally calm expression.

I looked back at Nix, whose eyes had closed. Her face was gray now, the Shadow's poison having traveled through her entire body.

Aidan landed heavily beside us, his golden wings casting a shadow over Nix. He shifted quickly, the flash of golden light giving way to his normal form. He knelt beside Nix, touched her arm gently.

Then his shoulders sagged.

A sob tore through my chest. I knew the words before he spoke them.

"There's nothing I can do. She is gone."

CHAPTER TWELVE

"No!" I leapt to my feet. "No!"

Cass jumped up, her eyes wild and desperate.

"I'm turning back time." I called my magic to me, letting my gift over time coil in my chest.

Draka rose quickly. "You mustn't. It's forbidden. Changing the past is too dangerous."

"It's only a minute." Cass's voice was hard. "Do it."

"What if you die?" Draka asked. "The Shadow could hit you with the same magic. Your Phantom form won't protect you."

I didn't care. I'd risk hell or eternal damnation or whatever it took to save Nix.

"I don't care." I met Cass's wild gaze. "Stop Nix from running."

Cass nodded firmly, her gaze set. "Do it now."

I raced back to where I'd stood with the other Shadow, fear shivering through my veins. Cass returned to her spot, Aidan took to the sky.

I met Draka's gaze. "Go back to the sky. It will help."

Worry and anger warred in her gaze, but she nodded, then shifted back into dragon form and took off. I'd never turned back the past with me and my friends in it—I'd only ever done it to my surroundings. I hoped it would help if everyone were close to the same position they had been, because honestly, I was floundering here.

But the sight of Nix's body firmed my resolve.

I dug deep for my magic, using my trick of envisioning at a ball of light inside my body. It was my mother's trick, I now knew. As I gathered the magic to the surface, I replayed my sword fight with the Shadow. I was going to have to be faster this time—but I knew what moves he would make.

Once I'd gathered up all my magic and all my control over time, I envisioned the moment before the Shadow cut my arm and my leg. I'd need all my strength and speed.

The magic poured out of me, twisting time and the space around me.

My skin chilled as time rewound itself. Shivers raced through me as I watched the world rewind. It happened in an instant, and then the Shadow with the sword was lunging for me.

He'd go for my left arm, I knew that now. I had to avoid the wounds, or I wouldn't be fast enough. I dodged right, narrowly avoiding his blow, and sank my blade deep into his gut.

Pond Flower appeared a moment later, but she stood off to the side, as if she knew this moment was somehow different. I kicked the Shadow off of my blade. I had only seconds until the barrier dropped.

The Shadow fell, crashing to the ground. I stabbed him one last time, through the neck, then looked up to see the other Shadow flicking his electric poisoned whip at the barrier of flame.

This would be the blow that destroyed the wall of fire. I raced toward it, desperate to reach him before he could flick out the second strike that would kill Nix or me.

Out of the corner of my eye, I saw Cass lunge for Nix and grab her. Cass's faith that I could handle this gave me strength.

As the barrier of flame dissipated fully, I lunged at the Shadow.

He drew back his arm to throw the killing strike, but I was too close. As I had before, I plunged my sword into his chest, then kicked him off the blade. This time, I followed it up with a slice to the throat as he fell. He was probably already close to death, but I was pissed and scared and wanted to finish the drill.

As he collapsed, his life force flowed away. I didn't spare him a glance, instead spinning around to find Cass and Nix.

Nix was struggling out of Cass's bear hug, confusion and annoyance on her face.

"What the hell, dude?" she demanded.

She'd just broken free when I hurtled toward her, throwing my arms around her and hugging her tight.

"Uh, thanks?" she said. Then she shoved me away.

I landed hard, crashing to my butt. Nix leapt over me and kicked a gray, muscular demon hard in the chest. He had a knife raised, as if he'd planned to stab me in the back. As he fell, Nix grabbed the knife, then followed him down to the ground, stabbing him in the neck. Blood sprayed her face, a gruesome war paint that somehow suited her.

I scrambled to my feet. The battle wasn't over. There were still demons left to fight. With the magical flame barrier gone, we were now exposed.

I powered up an icicle and sent it through the chest of a demon who was climbing over the edge of the platform. It plowed through his neck and sent him flying through the air. He disappeared far below.

Cass was throwing fireballs at the demons surrounding Claire, who fought like a banshee, her sword whirling so fast that it was a gray streak on the air. I joined in, hitting one with an icicle and another with a massive ball of ice to the head. He flew off the platform, his skull crushed.

On the other side of the platform, Connor was out of potion bombs. He fought with his infrequently-used sword, doing a pretty damned good job against a dark blue demon who was armed with an axe.

Airborne, Roarke and Aidan were polishing off the last of the demons who tried to climb onto the platform.

In the valley beyond, our side was winning.

By a landslide.

The demon bodies piled up, disappearing at different speeds as they returned to the Underworld where they belonged. Most of the living ones—a hundred at most—

were disappearing one at a time, using teleportation or transport charms. It was as if the Shadows' deaths and the carnage made them realize that this was just too damned dangerous.

On the western tundra, Mordaca and Aerdeca looted the bodies of the fallen demons. So did the rest of the Darklaners. I couldn't blame them. There was good loot to be found, and they deserved it. The Swamp Supes were doing the same, polishing off the last demons and searching the corpses before they disappeared. Some of the Order police looked on disapprovingly—anything found on the bodies should go to the Order, in their opinion—but they said nothing.

Today wasn't a day for sticking to the rules.

In the south, the monsters had started eating the demons. Prince Louie looked delighted, with blood flecking the curly white fur of one head and straight golden fur of the other as he chowed down on the corpses at his feet. I imagined that I saw bloodthirsty glee in the eyes of Ralph and Rufus, but they were too far away to confirm my suspicions.

Claire killed the last demon on the platform, and I joined Cass and Nix at the southern edge, where the last of the demons still fought. There were a few down below, at the very base, but the FireSouls were polishing them off.

I looked toward the mountains, grateful to see the healers moving onto the battlefield. There were at least a hundred and fifty of them, along with their assistants. Probably three hundred in total. It had been Roarke's idea to hire every healer we could find and bring them for the aftermath. They swarmed across the tundra, headed for the wounded.

"I think we've won," I said.

Cass looped an arm around my shoulder. "I think we have."

Nix grinned at us, her face painted with blood. "Good job, everyone!"

Cass winced and pointed to her cheek. "You've got a little something there. And there. And there."

"That demon had it coming."

Cass glanced at me. "Looks like Nix was determined to save you no matter what."

She had a point. And maybe that was the thing about changing the past. You couldn't change it very much. I'd only shifted it back a minute, but Nix had still found a way to save my life.

At least this time, she hadn't died.

I owed her a big thank you, and she didn't even realize. Or did she?

"Do you remember what happened?" I asked. If she did, she certainly wasn't making a big deal about it.

"With you saving me?" Nix said. "Yeah. I mean, I was confused at first. Then I realized you must have turned back time. I was dead, so I didn't see it. But I remember the rest of it. The poison, Cass hugging me weirdly."

"Thank you. You saved my life." Tears pricked my eyes.

She shrugged, but her gaze was fierce. "Or course."

She wasn't making a big deal about it. But I wasn't surprised. I'd done something similar over the summer and hadn't thought twice. It was just what we did for each other.

All the same, I reached out and hugged them both.

"Thanks, guys." The words were muffled by their hair, but they squeezed back. "I love you."

"Love you," Nix said.

"Love you too." Cass squeezed me one last time and let go.

As soon as she did, the aches and pains that I'd been able to ignore flared up. I may have avoided the Shadows' bigger hits, but the demons who'd come before them had gotten in some good jabs.

I sat down heavily, exhausted. Nix and Cass sat next to me. A closer inspection revealed that they were cut up and burned as well. Pond Flower, who looked unwounded, thank fates, flopped onto the ground in front of me, tongue lolling.

Roarke landed next to me. He was coated liberally in blood that gleamed darkly against his skin. There were cuts and gouges from claws, along with bite marks and a lump that was already swelling on his shoulder.

He smiled at me, his teeth white against his dark face. "You did it."

"We did it."

He nodded and sat, a wince twisting his features as his cuts made themselves known. Claire staggered over, along with Connor. They were leaning on each other, both looking like hell, and I was pretty sure that Connor's arm was hanging out of its socket.

Roarke noticed, too, and stood gingerly. "Let me get that for you, mate."

Connor nodded, looking vaguely ill. Roarke shoved the limb back into place. Connor gave a manly yelp, then sagged to the ground. Blood seeped from a head wound and various cuts, but he didn't look like he was going to pass out. Claire swayed, sitting beside him.

"I could use a beer," she said.

"Me too." This wasn't really a boxed wine situation.

"Soon enough." Roarke nodded to the battlefield behind me. "Our allies are coming."

I turned to look. Aidan was flying Corin and Alton over, while Mordaca and Aerdeca had hitched a ride on the back of a giant eagle. Zoya and Galina were riding up to the platform on a wave of snow, which was a neat trick, while Draka flew toward us through the white sky. Her translucent blue form was brilliant against the snow clouds. Prince Louie stood on his hind legs so that Emile could climb up onto the platform, and Cade landed next to us.

Everyone looked like hell, covered in cuts and burns, but at least they were all alive. They all took a seat in our makeshift circle, Draka in her human form. In the tundra beyond, their warriors packed up, helping the wounded off the battlefield.

"Were your casualties great?" I asked the group, worry twisting in my chest.

Galina shook her head. Her pale sparkling skin was blended with the white backdrop of the clouds. "Not many, no. Many were wounded, yes. But the demons were so distracted with trying to reach you, we could strike them from behind in most cases. By the time they realized what was going on, we were in a position for victory."

I nodded, relieved. "Good."

The plan had worked.

Mordaca shrugged elegantly, an unimpressed look on her face. "We only lost a few stupid ones, and that's because they stopped to loot the bodies too early."

"Greed will get you." Aerdeca wiped blood from her cheek, then rubbed it off on her pants. It blended right in with all the other blood. Her white outfit was entirely red, soaked with the blood of dozens of demons.

"The monsters are fine," Emile said. "Some cuts to legs and bellies, but nothing life-threatening. I only recruited the biggest, strongest ones. Most of them really enjoyed it, actually."

I grinned. I was glad for his foresight. I didn't want the deaths of the smaller animals on my hands.

"The Swamp Supes are pretty much good," Cade said. "Mostly because the demons thought they were on the same side."

"Excellent." I hadn't expected that, but it made sense. Most of those folks smelled like dark magic. Same for the Darklaners. That had probably protected them, too.

"The Order lost a few good mercenaries, from what I could see," Roarke said. "And there are a hell of a lot of injured."

I glanced back over my shoulder to check on the battlefield. The healers were kneeling by bodies, performing triage and transporting those with the worst wounds. Grief for those who were lost flared in my chest, but I was grateful it wasn't worse.

"No losses amongst the FireSouls." Corin leaned in and patted Pond Flower on the butt. "Thanks to the hellhounds, mostly. The demons couldn't get near us as long as we had a hellhound at our side."

"Good." I drew in a shaky breath, feeling weaker by the minute. I wouldn't pass out—I knew that feeling all to well—but the battle was starting to take its toll. "Thank you, everyone. You've saved us."

"We've saved us," Emile said. "It took everyone to finish the fight."

I smiled and nodded. They were right. Planning and friends had made this a success. And hopefully, we'd never have to fight a battle like this again.

That was cause for celebration. "We should have a party."

CHAPTER THIRTEEN

My parent's castle had never looked so good. It was sparkling and clean, all the color returned to it after the portal to hell had been closed. The chandeliers glittered, along with twinkle lights that had been strung all over the property. There were flowers and furniture, and the place even felt warmer.

It was a weird location for the party—travel was particularly difficult normally—but an appropriate one. Particularly given all that had happened.

After the battle, we'd all rested and gotten healed up. It'd taken about a week, since some of the injuries had turned out to be pretty bad. We'd then set about party planning and sent out invitations to everyone who'd fought. It was going to be a big crowd, which was one of the reasons I'd chosen this place. But I'd also wanted to claim it as my own and banish all the old ghosts.

My family had played a pivotal role in hatching the plot that had led to so many problems. But now they were all over. And we were waiting for the guests to arrive at a party to celebrate our victory. A special portal had been put in place, allowing people to transport directly into the courtyard if they had an invitation.

It was the perfect solution. As excited as I was for them to arrive, I was enjoying the peace and beauty of my old home now that it had been restored.

"You've done a good job." Draka's voice made me turn.

She was walking toward me in her human form, blue and glowing. Pride shined on her face. For me? My heart warmed.

"Thank you," I said. "Though I wish some things had been different. That I'd never opened the portal to Oriamor at all. But I'm glad it's over."

"You know that you had no choice in opening the portal. It was fated. Even the Ice Fae had a prophecy about it."

Her words made me feel a bit better.

On the side of the room, Connor fiddled with the speakers. Music began to fill the room.

"Thank you for all of your help," I said.

Draka smiled. "My pleasure. I'll always be there for you, Del."

"Well, I hope I won't need too much help, but that you'll continue to come see me."

"Of course I will." She reached out and hugged me.

I gripped her tight. For most of my life, she was the closest thing to a mother I'd had.

She stepped away, then gestured to the wall behind me. "There is someone waiting for you."

I turned, confusion flaring into disbelief. My parents stood against the wall, looking uncertain and out of place. They were hazy and transparent—ghosts, most definitely—but they were here. I looked back at Draka. "You're sticking around?"

She nodded. "Go to them. They want to see you."

I wanted to see them, too, though it felt kind of weird, given everything that had happened.

"I love you, Draka," I said.

She smiled. "I love you too. Now go."

I nodded and turned, walking over to my parents. Up close, they looked even more uncertain. They were wearing old-fashioned clothes, and my father had the same beard and piercing eyes that I remembered. My mother looked the same as when I'd seen her before.

"How are you here?" I asked.

"We've received special permission to haunt this place occasionally," my mother said.

I laughed, unable to help myself. "That's a thing?"

"Yes. When one has unfinished business."

"What's your unfinished business?" Hope for something that I didn't even understand filled my chest.

"Having a relationship with you," my father said.

Shock pierced me. "What? I—I—"

"Don't know if you even want that?" my mother asked.

Exactly. Though didn't I want that? I'd always wanted it—a good relationship with parents who loved me.

"But you guys gave me to the Monster," I said. "He locked me in a dungeon. And you wanted to use me in a plot to destroy the world. I mean, that's even worse than stuff on daytime TV."

Sadness shined in my parents' eyes. My head spun. This was surreal and strange, and I had no idea how to process it.

"We were wrong," my father said. "We realize that now. The portal—"

"I know. Twisted your minds with dark magic. But it didn't twist my mind. Why were you susceptible."

"You are rare, Del." My mother's gaze was full of pride, just like Draka's had been. "Strong and brave and fated to save the world. You could never be susceptible to something like that."

I liked her words, but they still left me confused.

"We understand that we're not going to be a normal, happy family," my father said. A small grin tugged at his mouth. "For one, we're dead. We can come here occasionally, but we're still ghosts. But if you're willing to give us a second chance, we're here for that. We want that."

"So badly." Tears gleamed in my mother's eyes.

I didn't know what to say, nor what I truly wanted, but I did believe them. If I wanted a relationship with them, I could have it. That was something I'd figure out later, though, when things had settled down.

"Thank you," I said. "I'm glad that you're seeing things differently now."

"So are we." My mother reached out and hugged me. Her touch was warm and soft despite her ghostly form. "I love you, Delphine."

My father hugged us both. "I love you, Delphine."

"I love you both." I hugged them back, then stepped away.

"We must go now, but if you come back, we can visit you again," my mother said.

I nodded. Though I was still confused, I had the distinct feeling that I would work on forgiving them.

They waved, then drifted away, out of the room.

"That looked like it went well."

Roarke's voice made me turn. He looked so handsome that I couldn't look anywhere else.

I smiled. "I think it did."

"I have some more good news. I spoke to the Order of the Magica. Their mercenaries witnessed some pretty intense power on your part."

Nerves tightened my skin. They still didn't know I was a FireSoul, or the true extent of my powers. They wouldn't like it. "And?"

"And they've agreed to not question you." His gaze hardened. "At my strong suggestion. They don't know exactly what you are, and they won't ask. Though they are wary of the extent of your power—especially since they don't know much about it—you were clearly willing to sacrifice yourself to save everyone. Because of that, they've agreed to drop the matter. And they will pardon anyone who was a fugitive before the battle, like Emile."

A smile spread across my face. Emile had been hiding from the Order since we'd busted him out of their prison a few months ago. Now, he was a free man. And I was off the Order's radar. Temporarily, at least. Either way, they had to like me at least a little now.

"You're the best." I threw myself at Roarke, wrapping my arms around his neck and leaning up to kiss him.

Happiness flowed through me as his lips moved expertly on mine. I fell into the kiss, temporarily losing my mind as his lips moved on mine. We'd spent the last week living in both our houses, with Pond Flower stopping in for frequent visits. It'd been amazing. Just like his kiss.

"Chill out, guys." Nix's voice broke my concentration.

I pulled away from Roarke.

Nix grinned, her green eyes bright and so familiar. I was so damned grateful she was alive. I didn't always love my weird powers, but I was thankful for them. Especially now.

"Guests are starting to arrive." Nix hiked a thumb toward the main entrance. The courtyard is filling up fast. Dr. Garriso is here, along with some crazy lady wearing a rainbow-sequined jumpsuit. And so are the FireSouls, and Aerdeca and Mordaca. Emile brought the dog Prince Louie. I think it's time for the party to start."

"It's definitely time." Cass approached, a can of her favorite PBR in her hand.

She had believed in me when I'd had to turn back time to save Nix. She'd always believe in me.

I loved both my *deirfiúr* so much.

"There's already dancing," Cass said. "And the Swamp Supes have brought their own band. They're all covered in slime. Should they be allowed in the house?"

"Sure." I shrugged. After all the darkness this place had seen, a slimy fiddle player wasn't a problem. "Let's get this party started."

As a group, we walked toward the main doors to let the crowd into the house. Aidan joined us, along with Connor and Claire. As I pulled open the doors to welcome everyone to the party, I couldn't help but marvel at my good fortune. Joy like I'd never known flowed through me. My life hadn't been easy, but it'd given me *everything*.

THANK YOU FOR READING!

I hope you enjoyed reading this book as much as I enjoyed writing it. Reviews are so helpful to authors. I really appreciate all reviews, both positive and negative. If you want to leave one, you can do so at Amazon or GoodReads.

If you liked Aleta Indigo, the mysterious girl who helped Del in the cemetery, you can read more about her in Alison Claire's upcoming series, Hell's Belles. It looks like it's going to be fabulous. Check out the author's note for more info.

AUTHOR'S NOTE

Thank you so much for reading *Phantom Magic!* As with all of my books, I included historical and mythological elements. If you're interested in reading more about that, read on. At the end, I'll talk a bit about why Del and her *deirfiúr* are treasure hunters and how I try to make that fit with archaeology's ethics (which don't condone treasure hunting, as I'm sure you might have guessed). I spoke about this in the Author's Notes for the other books in the series, so if you've read any of those, then you've read this. But it's important stuff, so I wanted to include it here for anyone who missed it before.

First—a fun new thing. You may have noticed that Southern folklore played a big part in the beginning of *Phantom Magic.* The character Aleta Indigo was borrowed from fellow author Alison Claire, who knows more about Southern history and folklore than I will ever know. She's written a fabulous series called Hell's Belles that will come out in early summer 2017 that's all about a group of badass magical debutantes in Savannah, Georgia. They'll bless your heart and then hex your ass, as Alison would say.

Aleta Indigo is one of those characters and I was lucky enough to read a sneak peek that made me fall madly in love. Alison was kind enough to let Aleta make an appearance in *Phantom Magic*. I love how it expands the worlds in both series. If you'd like to read a free book featuring Aleta Indigo and her fellow witches, visit smarturl.it/Belles.

Now, onto the history in *Phantom Magic*! There isn't quite as much as in other books, but it's some of my favorite. Bonaventure cemetery, the setting for the second scene in *Phantom Magic*, is a real place in Savannah Georgia. In the day, it's incredibly beautiful, but at night... Well, it's very spooky, as I'm sure you can imagine. It's situated right on the river with hundreds of Live Oaks dripping Spanish moss. The local historical society offers wonderful tours. One of those tours gave me the inspiration to set a scene there.

There are many famous southerners buried at Bonaventure. In fact, it was *the* place to be buried in the 19th century. So popular, in fact, that people would have their loved ones exhumed from less famous cemeteries and reburied at Bonaventure just so that they could say they had a relative there. It was major social currency.

However, given the history of the American South, some of the people buried in the cemetery were pretty bad individuals. Don't get me wrong—the South has many great qualities. I've lived there most of my life and love it. But there is a dark history with slavery that can't be denied. In the *Phantom Magic*, there was a very brief scene where Del notices a male ghost being chased around his sarcophagus by some other ghosts. While touring the cemetery, I learned of a horrible man who sold young girls as slaves. He had the most magnificent sarcophagus, no doubt paid for by his terrible career. Frankly, it pissed me off. So I resurrected him in this book and gave him a terrible afterlife of being constantly chased around his own coffin. Perhaps the other ghosts catch him, but I'll leave that up to you to decide.

Bonaventure Cemetery, and the area surrounding it, provided quite a lot of inspiration for the mythological elements in the story. The two primary ones are Haints and Boo Hags. Both of these mythological figures come from the Gullah Culture in the American South. The Gullah people are the descendants of slaves brought from West Africa for their knowledge of rice-growing techniques. Though they once lived in an area stretching from North Carolina down to Florida, they presently live in South Carolina and Georgia, specifically, near the coast. They've always had a strong community culture, which has allowed them to preserve a lot of their African heritage and early American heritage.

The Gullah people's folklore includes tales of Haints and Boo Hags. Haints are the spirits of the dead, and the origin of the word may come from the word 'haunt'. Haints are said to be unable to cross water. One fascinating tidbit that was mentioned very briefly in the story was the color Haint Blue. It is generally a shade of light blue that is painted around doors and windows and even on porch ceilings. This color was used all over the American South to prevent Haints from entering the houses because the Haint would think the paint was water and they would turn back and not enter your house. In the story, Aleta Indigo (the Spooky Southern Superman) tells the woman who had been attacked by the Boo Hag to paint her windowsills and porch ceiling blue to protect herself in the future.

Which brings us to Boo Hags (or just Hags, for short). Boo Hags are also put off by the color Haint Blue. They are witches who look like people during the day (usually like a beautiful woman), but at night, they shed their skin and sneak into people's homes to steal their energy by sucking some of the life force from them while they sleep. The person doesn't die from this, though they will wake tired. However, if you struggle, the Boo Hag will decide that you are not worth her time and she will steal your skin (then you die). Boo Hags usually crouch over their victims while sucking their life force, which led to the phrase "Don't let de hag ride ya!". The only way to kill a Boo Hag is to find and destroy its skin, or to distract the Boo Hag from finding its skin before sunrise. This distraction can also protect you while you are sleeping. Boo Hags like to count things, so if you want to protect yourself and have a shot at killing the Boo Hag, leave a broom by your bed and they will be compelled to count the bristles. If you're lucky, they'll still be counting at sunrise and won't have time to make it to their skin. Then, you're rid of that Boo Hag forever.

That's it for the historical influences in *Phantom Magic*. However, one of the most important things about this book is how Del and her *deirfiúr* treat artifacts and their business, Ancient Magic. This is the part of the Author's Note that is written in the other books, so if you've read any of those, this'll be a repeat. But it's important enough that I like to include it in all my books. My conscience wouldn't rest otherwise.

As I'm sure you know, archaeology isn't quite like Indiana Jones (for which I'm both grateful and bitterly disappointed). Sure, it's exciting and full of travel. However, booby-traps are not as common as I expected. Total number of booby-traps I have encountered in my career: zero. Still hoping, though.

When I chose to write a series about archaeology and treasure hunting, I knew I had a careful line to tread. There is a big difference between these two activities. As much as I value artifacts, they are not treasure. Not even the gold artifacts. They are pieces of our history that contain valuable information, and as such, they belong to all of us. Every artifact that is excavated should be properly conserved and stored in a museum so that everyone can have access to our history. No one single person can own history, and I believe very strongly that individuals should not own artifacts. Treasure hunting is the pursuit of artifacts for personal gain.

So why did I make Del and her *deirfiúr* treasure hunters? I'd have loved to call them archaeologists, but nothing about Cass's work is like archaeology. Archaeology is a very laborious, painstaking process— and it certainly doesn't involve selling artifacts. That wouldn't work for the fast-paced, adventurous series that I had planned for *Dragon's Gift*. Not to mention the fact that dragons are famous for coveting treasure. Considering where the *deirfiúr* got their skills from, it just made sense to call them treasure hunters.

Even though I write urban fantasy, I strive for accuracy. The *deirfiúr* don't engage in archaeological practices—therefore, I cannot call them archaeologists. I also have a duty as an archaeologist to properly represent my field and our goals—namely, to protect and share history. Treasure hunting doesn't do this. One of the biggest battles that archaeology faces today is protecting cultural heritage from thieves.

I debated long and hard about not only what to call the heroines of this series, but also about how they would do their jobs. I wanted it to involve all the cool things we think about when we think about archaeology—namely, the Indiana Jones stuff, whether it's real or not. But I didn't know quite how to do that while still staying within the bounds of my own ethics. I can cut myself and other writers some slack because this is fiction, but I couldn't go too far into smash and grab treasure hunting.

I consulted some of my archaeology colleagues to get their take, which was immensely helpful. Wayne Lusardi, the State Maritime Archaeologist for Michigan, and Douglas Inglis and Veronica Morris, both archaeologists for Interactive Heritage, were immensely helpful with ideas. My biggest problem was figuring out how to have the heroines steal artifacts from tombs and then sell them and still sleep at night. Everything I've just said is pretty counter to this, right?

That's where the magic comes in. The heroines aren't after the artifacts themselves (they put them back where they found them, if you recall)—they're after the magic that the artifacts contain. They're more like magic hunters than treasure hunters. That solved a big part of my problem. At least they were putting the artifacts back. Though that's not proper archaeology, I could let it pass. At least it's clear that they believe they shouldn't keep the artifact or harm the site. But the SuperNerd in me said, "Well, that magic is part of the artifact's context. It's important to the artifact and shouldn't be removed and sold."

Now *that* was a problem. I couldn't escape my SuperNerd self, so I was in a real conundrum. Fortunately, that's where the immensely intelligent Wayne Lusardi came in. He suggested that the magic could have an expiration date. If the magic wasn't used before it decayed, it could cause huge problems. Think explosions and tornado spells run amok. It could ruin the entire site, not to mention possibly cause injury and death. That would be very bad.

So now you see why Del and her *deirfiúr* don't just steal artifacts to sell them. Not only is selling the magic cooler, it's also better from an ethical standpoint, especially if the magic was going to cause problems in the long run. These aren't perfect solutions—the perfect solution would be sending in a team of archaeologists to carefully record the site and remove the dangerous magic—but that wouldn't be a very fun book.

Thanks again for reading (especially if you got this far!). I hope you enjoyed the story and will stick with Del on the rest of her adventure!

ACKNOWLEDGMENTS

Thank you, Ben, for everything. There would be no books without you.

Thank you to fellow urban fantasy author Alison Claire, for letting me use the character Aleta Indigo from your Hell's Belles series. She gave the Bonaventure Cemetery scene something special.

Thank you to Lindsey Loucks for your excellent editing. The book is immensely better because of you! And thank you to Crystal Jeffs, for your help with continuity in the book. You remember things better than I do, and it's definitely a better story because of you! Thank you to Rebecca Frank for the beautiful cover. You really bring Del to life.

And thank you to Aisha Panjeweeany, first for finding typos in the book (you have a very keen eye), and second for suggesting the band name Alien Panda Jury. It is a band based out of Pakistan created by musician Daniel Arthur Panjwaneey. I chose to use the band name because it's awesome, but then I listened to the music, which is even better.

The Dragon's Gift series is a product of my two lives: one as an archaeologist and one as a novelist. Combining these two took a bit of work. I'd like to thank my friends, Wayne Lusardi, the State Maritime Archaeologist for Michigan, and Douglas Inglis and Veronica Morris, both archaeologists for Interactive Heritage, for their ideas about how to have a treasure hunter heroine that doesn't conflict too much with archaeology's ethics. The

Author's Note contains a bit more about this if you are interested.

GLOSSARY

Alpha Council - There are two governments that enforce law for supernaturals—the Alpha Council and the Order of the Magica. The Alpha Council governs all shifters. They work cooperatively with Alpha Council when necessary - for example, when capturing FireSouls.

Blood Sorceress - A type of Magica who can create magic using blood.

Boo Hag - A witch from Gullah culture. She will sneak into your house and suck out your energy.

Conjurer - A Magica who uses magic to create something from nothing. They cannot create magic, but if there is magic around them, they can put that magic into their conjuration.

Dark Magic - The kind that is meant to harm. It's not necessarily bad, but it often is.

Deirfiúr - Sisters in Irish.

Demons - Often employed to do evil. They live in various hells but can be released upon the earth if you know how to get to them and then get them out. If they are killed on Earth, they are sent back to their hell.

Dragon Sense - A FireSoul's ability to find treasure. It is an internal sense that pulls them toward what they seek. It is easiest to find gold, but they can find anything or anyone that is valued by someone.

Elemental Mage – A rare type of mage who can manipulate all of the elements.

Enchanted Artifacts – Artifacts can be imbued with magic that lasts after the death of the person who put the magic into the artifact (unlike a spell that has not been put into an artifact—these spells disappear after the Magica's death). But magic is not stable. After a period of time—hundreds or thousands of years depending on the circumstance—the magic will degrade. Eventually, it can go bad and cause many problems.

Fire Mage – A mage who can control fire.

FireSoul - A very rare type of Magica who shares a piece of the dragon's soul. They can locate treasure and steal the gifts (powers) of other supernaturals. With practice, they can manipulate the gifts they steal, becoming the strongest of that gift. They are despised and feared. If they are caught, they are thrown in the Prison of Magical Deviants.

The Great Peace - The most powerful piece of magic ever created. It hides magic from the eyes of humans.

Haints - A ghost from Gullah culture.

Hearth Witch – A Magica who is versed in magic relating to hearth and home. They are often good at potions and protective spells and are also very perceptive when on their own turf.

Magica - Any supernatural who has the power to create magic—witches, sorcerers, mages. All are governed by the Order of the Magica.

Mirror Mage - A Magica who can temporarily borrow the powers of other supernaturals. They can mimic the powers as long as they are near the other supernatural. Or they can hold on to the power, but once they are away from the other supernatural, they can only use it once.

The Origin - The descendent of the original alpha shifter. They are the most powerful shifter and can turn into any species.

Order of the Magica - There are two governments that enforce law for supernaturals—the Alpha Council and the Order of the Magica. The Order of the Magica govern all Magica. They work cooperatively with the Alpha Council when necessary - for example, when capturing FireSouls.

Phantom - A type of supernatural that is similar to a ghost. They are incorporeal. They feed off the misery and pain of others, forcing them to relive their greatest nightmares and fears. They do not have a fully functioning mind like a human or supernatural. Rather, they are a shadow of their former selves. Half bloods are extraordinarily rare.

Seeker - A type of supernatural who can find things. FireSouls often pass off their dragon sense as Seeker power.

Shifter - A supernatural who can turn into an animal. All are governed by the Alpha Council.

Transporter - A type of supernatural who can travel anywhere. Their power is limited and must regenerate after each use.

Warden of the Underworld - A one of a kind position created by Roarke. He keeps order in the Underworld.

ABOUT LINSEY

Before becoming a writer, Linsey Hall was a nautical archaeologist who studied shipwrecks from Hawaii and the Yukon to the UK and the Mediterranean. She credits fantasy and historical romances with her love of history and her career as an archaeologist. After a decade of tromping around the globe in search of old bits of stuff that people left lying about, she settled down and started penning her own romance novels. Her Dragon's Gift series draws upon her love of history and the paranormal elements that she can't help but include.

Copyright 2017 by Linsey Hall
Published by Bonnie Doon Press LLC

Linsey@LinseyHall.com
www.LinseyHall.com
https://twitter.com/HiLinseyHall
https://www.facebook.com/LinseyHallAuthor

BONNIE
DOON
PRESS

ISBN 978-1-942085-46-1

Printed in Great Britain
by Amazon